SHOTGUN

This Large Print Book carries the
Seal of Approval of N.A.V.H.

SHOTGUN

ELMER KELTON

THORNDIKE PRESS

An imprint of Thomson Gale, a part of The Thomson Corporation

THOMSON
GALE™

Detroit • New York • San Francisco • New Haven, Conn. • Waterville, Maine • London

THOMSON

★ ™

GALE

LIBRARY OF CONGRESS CATALOGING-IN-PUBLICATION DATA

Kelton, Elmer.
 Shotgun / by Elmer Kelton.
  p. cm. — (Thorndike Press large print Western)
 "Originally published in 1969 by Paperback Library as Shotgun Settlement by Alex Hawk, a pseudonym of Elmer Kelton"—T.p. verso.
 ISBN-13: 978-0-7862-9558-6 (hardcover : alk. paper)
 ISBN-10: 0-7862-9558-9 (hardcover : alk. paper)
 1. Texas, West — Fiction. 2. Large type books. I. Hawk, Alex, 1926–Shotgun settlement. II. Title.
PS3561.E3975S48 2007
813'.54—dc22   2007014956

Published in 2007 by arrangement with Tom Doherty Associates, LLC.

Printed in the United States of America on permanent paper
10 9 8 7 6 5 4 3 2 1

SHOTGUN

I

The hostler at the Two Forks Livery & Grain paused in his listless pitching of hay as he saw two riders move down from the crest of the limestone hill. Harley Mills rubbed a sleeve over his sweat-streaked face and speculated as to whether he was fixing to get some customers. Hot as it was, and seeing as the stable didn't belong to him, he had as soon not have business get out of hand. It hadn't lately. With this drought on, people were playing it close to their belts. They weren't coming to town when they didn't have to, because money was tight. He went back to his halfhearted efforts until one of the horses in the corral thrust its head over the top plank and nickered. An answer came from out on the road. Mills put the hayfork aside and stepped through the gate.

The two men were strangers to him. "Mornin'," he said. "From the looks of the dust on you, you've come a ways. I expect them horses could stand a feed."

No one replied. The hostler stared a moment at a rust-bearded man hunched on a streak-faced bay, then his reddish eyes were drawn to the taller rider, a gaunt, sallow-faced man who studied him in dark distrust. The hostler felt a sudden misgiving and wished they had passed him by.

The man said, "You're Harley Mills."

The hostler swallowed, puzzled. "That's right. But I don't know you. Or do I?"

The rider said, "You didn't used to swamp stables. Time I remember you, you was cowboyin' for old man Blair Bishop."

"Used to. He fired — we come to a partin', years ago." Harley Mills searched the seldom-explored recesses of his whiskey-dimmed memory. Something in those deep-set black eyes reached him. His jaw dropped.

The rider responded with a hard grin. "Know me now, don't you?"

Mills nodded, dry-mouthed and nervous.

The tall man said evenly, "Then I reckon we'll leave these horses with you. Me and Owen, we're goin' to go wash some of the dust down. You take good care of them now, Harley, you hear? Good care." Mills could only nod. The tall rider swung to the hoof-scuffed ground and shoved the leather reins into Mills' numb hands. He reached back to his warbag tied behind the saddle and fetched out a cartridge belt. He took his time putting it on while the hostler stared at the .45 in fearful fascination.

The man asked, "Things ain't changed much in ten years, have they?" Mills shook his head, a knot in his throat. The rider queried, "Blair Bishop still figurin' hisself the big he-coon?" The hostler's eyes gave him the answer and he added, "Well, things can't stay the same forever. Come on, Owen, we're past due for that drink."

Harley Mills barely glanced at the red-bearded Owen as he took the second set of reins. He watched the tall man stride up the street, looking at first one side of it, then the other. Mills led the horses into the corral, slipped the saddles and bridles off and gave the mounts a good bait of oats. His fingers touched a saddlegun in a scabbard as he swung the tall man's saddle onto a rack, and he jerked his hand back as if he had touched a hot stove.

Done, he shut the corral gate behind him and struck a stiff trot up the street to the courthouse. He almost ran down the county clerk as he rushed through the hall and into the door of the sheriff's office. He gestured excitedly at the graying ex-cowboy who looked up startled from his paperwork.

"It's Macy Modock," he blurted, gasping for breath. "Macy Modock is back in town."

The sheriff poked his head through the door of the Two Forks Bar & Billiard Emporium. Looking around quickly, he spotted the two men seated at a small table. He stared a moment, his heavy fingers gripping the doorjamb. At length the tall man spoke to him. "Come on in, Erly. Wondered how long it would take you."

Sheriff Erly Greenwood moved solemnly, his sun-browned face pinched into a frown. He halted two paces from the table, gave the red-bearded man a quick glance, then gazed at the other. "What you doin' here, Macy?"

"Havin' a drink. Share a little sunshine with us?"

"You was in the pen, Macy. How come you out?"

"I was turned out. Got all the proper papers right here in my pocket." He tapped his shirt. "Care to look?"

The sheriff nodded. "Maybe I better." His frown deepened, and his moustache worked a little as he read. "You didn't serve out all the term they gave you."

10

"Good behavior, Erly. Surprise you I could behave myself?"

"Damn sure does. I figured you'd get in a fight and some other prisoner would stomp your brains out. Hoped so, as a matter of fact."

"But here I am back in Two Forks, like a bad penny."

"I want you out, Macy. Have your drink, get your horses fed, then ride on out. I don't want to ever see you again . . . not in this town, not in this country."

Macy Modock studied his half-finished drink, a little anger flaring before he quickly forced it back. "Erly, if you'll read that paper a little closer you'll see it says I done paid up all I owe. I can come and go as I please, here or anywhere else. And after all, I'm a property owner in Two Forks. I come to see about my property."

"After ten years? That old saloon you had is half fallen in. Kids broke out all the windowlights the first week you was gone. Wind took off most of the shingles, and rain has done the rest."

"The land it sets on is mine. I come to see after my property. There can't nobody quarrel over that."

Erly Greenwood shifted his weight from one foot to the other. His jaw worked, but it was a while before any words came out. "Macy, we've had a nice quiet town here the last few years."

Modock nodded. "You're puttin' on some belly."

"Just you listen to what I tell you. If you've come to settle up any old scores, I won't have it."

A hard smile came to Macy Modock's thin, cheek-sunken face. "I got no grudge against you, Erly. You just done what you was told. The boss man snapped his fingers and you jumped. That's how it always was, them days. He still snappin' his fingers, Erly?"

Anger leaped into Erly Greenwood's face. "He's a good man, Macy. Anything he done to you, he done for good cause. If you've come back to raise hell . . ."

Macy Modock glanced at his red-whiskered companion. "Like I told you, Owen, things ain't really changed. The years go by, people get older, but everything else stays the same."

The sheriff's voice carried an edge. "I want you out of here."

"When I get ready. Who knows? I might take a notion to rebuild."

Conviction came to Erly Greenwood. "You've come to get even with him, Macy.

Don't you try."

Modock grunted. "You was just a cowboy when Blair Bishop had that badge pinned on you. You're still just a cowboy."

"That's a matter of opinion. Don't you crowd me."

Modock stared at him coldly. "If there's trouble between me and Blair Bishop, it'll be when he comes huntin' me, not me huntin' him."

Macy Modock turned away from the sheriff. He poured himself a fresh drink and held it in his hand, admiring the amber color as if he had dismissed the sheriff from his mind. Greenwood turned on his heel and left.

The smile came back slowly to Modock's line-creased mouth. "And Blair Bishop *will* come huntin' me, Owen. I'll *make* him hunt me. And when I shoot him in self-defense, not even a Two Forks jury can touch me."

II

Blair Bishop lay on his back beneath the lacy shade of a tall mesquite tree and rubbed his right hand. Why was it, he wondered ruefully, that when a man got of an age where he ought to be able to stand back and breathe good, enjoy what he had built for himself and take the pleasure of turning responsibilities over to his sons, he had to start putting up with things like rheumatism? If it wasn't in his hands, it was in his hips. If it wasn't in his hips, it was in his legs. There wasn't a part of his body that hadn't at one time or another been fallen on, rolled over or kicked by a horse.

He looked past his big gray mount, tied to a limb of the mesquite. "See anything yet, Hez?"

Hez Northcutt, sitting on a leggy dun, stood in his stirrups and squinted. "Somebody's comin'. Looks like it's probably Finn

14

bringin' old Clarence and that sorry crew of his."

Blair Bishop pushed slowly to his feet, wincing a little as a rheumatism pain lanced through his hip. Damn it, he wasn't too far past fifty. A man ought not to have to put up with this till he was old. He took off his hat and rubbed a sleeve across his sweaty brow, then pulled the spotted old Stetson down firmly over his thick gray hair. He squinted toward a wire corral full of bawling cows and restless calves, the dust rising thick and brown and drifting away in the hot west wind. This was a corral he used twice a year in branding the Double B onto his cattle that ranged this part of his land. But the cattle in the pen didn't wear that brand. They carried a C Bar. They were thin, their ribs showing through.

This had been a hard year for all cattle, Bishop's and everybody's. Beyond the corral, stretching for miles and disappearing into the shimmering heatwaves, lay grassland brown and short, thirsting for rain. The only thing green was the mesquite trees, which had deep roots and could outlast any other living plant except the cactus.

August had come, and it hadn't rained since March. Even that had been little more than a shower, following a dry winter. The brass of the summer sky showed little sign it would yield up rain for a long time yet.

Young Hez Northcutt slipped a pistol out of its holster and spun the cylinder, checking the load. "Hez," Blair spoke gently, "you can put that thing up. You'll have no use for it today."

Hez looked at him dubiously, plainly hoping. "You sure, Mister Bishop?"

"Clarence Cass will threaten and whine, but he wouldn't fight a blind jackrabbit. And them boys with him, they're just on a payroll. They won't bloody theirselves for the likes of Clarence."

The cowboy put the pistol away.

From behind the corral, where he had been looking over the cows, another young man rode up on a stocking-legged sorrel. He turned his gaze a moment toward the dust rising on the wagon road, then looked down regretfully at the broad-shouldered rancher. "Dad, we're treatin' old Clarence awful rough."

"Clarence Cass is a user, boy. He's like a parasite tick that gets on a cow's ear and sucks blood till it busts itself. He'll use you for all he can get out of you and then complain because you didn't give him more. Now and again you got to treat him rough. It's the only way you can tell him no."

Allan Bishop drummed his hand against his saddle horn. His voice was testy. "Still looks like we could've gone and talked to him."

Blair Bishop put his hands on his hips and leaned back, stretching, wishing he could work the rheumatism out. Impatience touched him, but he tried not to let it take over. Hell, the boy wasn't but twenty-two. At that age, even Blair had still harbored notions about the inherent goodness of all men, goodness that would just naturally come out of its own accord if you would but reason with them. Blair Bishop had eventually had all such notions stomped out of him. His son hadn't, yet. Blair knew some men had it in them to do the right thing, and some didn't. The latter you had just as well not waste your time with. Minute you turned your back to them they would be whittling on you.

Blair thought his son made a good picture sitting there in the saddle. Strong shoulders, straight back, an earnest young face and square chin. In a lot of ways he looked like Blair had looked, maybe twenty-five years ago. Except Blair had never been that handsome the best day he had ever lived. Allan had inherited some looks from his mother's side.

And a little contrariness, too, Blair thought. It never come from me; I never been contrary in my life.

"Allan, one of these days this place will belong to you and your brother, Billy. He's too young yet to take on the tough end of it, but you're not. You know as well as I do that we've tried talkin' reason to old Clarence. Now it's your place to stand with me when we *show* the old beggar."

Allan's jaw was set hard.

Blair shrugged, losing patience. "All right, let's talk straight. It ain't old Clarence you're thinkin' about; it's that girl of his. Forget it, boy."

"Anything that hurts the old man hurts Jessie."

"So it'll just have to hurt her. You better forget about her, boy. She won't bring you nothin' but problems."

"You don't know her."

"I know the old man. I never knew the girl's mother, but I expect if she was much she never would've married Clarence. I been a stockman all my life. I know that if you breed a scrubby stud to a scrubby mare, you get a scrubby colt."

Anger leaped into Allan's face and he pulled his horse away, turning his back on his father.

Blair clenched his teeth. Maybe he oughtn't to've talked so rough, but he knew no way except being blunt. Though people didn't always agree with Blair Bishop, they never misunderstood him. He watched silently as his son moved the sorrel down the wagon road to meet the oncoming riders.

Hez Northcutt said: "I'm about his age, Mister Bishop. Maybe *I* can talk to him."

Blair shook his head. The cowboy had a point, but Blair rejected it. Blair had long had an easy partnership with both his sons. He still had it with Billy, who was about fifteen. But somehow the last couple or three years he had lost that open-handed relationship with Allan. At a time when two men ought to draw closer together, why was it they tended instead to pull apart? Why was it a father had to become a stranger to a son?

"He'll come around," Blair told the cowboy. "Just stubborn. Got that from his mother, God rest her."

Blair's foreman, Finn Goforth, spurred ahead of the riders so he could reach Blair Bishop first. On the way he passed Allan, and he spoke to him. If Allan replied, Blair couldn't tell it. Finn, fortyish and graying, took a curious glance back over his shoulder at Allan. "I fetched them, Mister Bishop."

"How did Clarence take it?"

"Like we'd poured coal oil in his whiskey barrel. He's bellyached all the way over here. I'll let you listen to him now; I'm sick of it."

Blair said, "I didn't figure on listenin'. I figured on doin' the talkin'." He scowled, watching his son pull up even with the Cass girl. "I wish I could talk to *him*," he complained.

"Allan's full growed," Finn commented. "You've always taught him to think for himself. You wouldn't give three cents for him if he didn't."

"Sure, I want him to think for himself," Blair said. "But I want him to think like *I* do."

Skinny Clarence Cass rode in front, hunched over in his saddle like a loose sack of bran. A short way behind him came a girl on a sidesaddle, her long dark skirt covering all but the ankles of her leather boots. Bringing up the rear were two Cass cowboys, in no hurry at all. Blair Bishop watched his son talking to the girl. At the distance he couldn't hear, but Allan's gestures made it plain he was apologizing.

Blair could tell by the pinch of Clarence's shoulders that the little man was fit to chew

20

a horseshoe up and spit it out. A humorless smile came to Blair as he took a few steps forward. "Howdy, Clarence."

Cass reined up, his face splotched red from anger and the heat of the ride. "Bishop . . ." He had a thin neck, wattled like a turkey's.

Blair found himself smiling a little broader. He was actually enjoying this confrontation, and the realization surprised him a little. "I do believe we've got some of your cattle in that pen yonder."

Clarence Cass' anger was too much for him to hold. "Blair, you're a harsh man and a poor neighbor. An occasional beef critter of mine strays over onto your land and you abuse them and me like you was the Lord Almighty. One of these days you'll overstep yourself."

"There's more than an occasional critter in that pen; count them yourself. There's somethin' past a hundred head. And they didn't drift. Finn and Hez found where they was pushed through a cut fence. There was footprints all around where that wire was pinched. Cass footprints, I'd judge."

Cass blustered. "You got no proof of that."

"A man needs proof for court. I ain't goin' to court. I'm holdin' court of my own." Bishop's smile was suddenly gone. "Now

21

you listen to me, Clarence, because I'm only goin' to tell you once and I don't want you to ever say you didn't hear. Your country is overstocked; I tried to tell you that last spring. Now your cows have eaten off all your grass and drunk up most of your water. You're tryin' to get them through by havin' them take mine. But I got barely enough to see my own cattle through till fall, and if it don't rain by then I'm in trouble same as you are."

For a moment he was distracted by sight of Jessie Cass. He saw her open her mouth as if to speak, then drop her chin. Well, he thought, at least she's got the decency to feel shame over the stunt her father tried to pull. Blair saw his son reach out and take Jessie's hand and squeeze it, reassuring her. "Damn it, boy," he wanted to say, "we got to stick together on this thing." But he couldn't rebuke his son in the presence of Cass and his crew; it would demean them both. He would wait.

He turned back to Cass. "Now you listen to me, Clarence. You've had all the free grass and free water you're goin' to steal from the Bishops. From this day on, we're goin' to watch our fences close. Any of your cattle we find over here, we'll run till they're ready to drop. For ever dollar's worth of grass you steal, you'll lose five dollars worth of beef. We'll run them till there's no run left in them, then we'll put them back across the fence. Now, you think you can remember that?"

Clarence Cass looked as if he was about to suffer a stroke. He tried to argue, but he couldn't. He tried to curse, but only a half-intelligible gibberish came out. His Adam's apple bobbed up and down in anger and frustration, but he sat there and took Blair's tongue-lashing without striking back.

Blair glanced at the two Cass cowboys, not expecting any trouble from them. Cass didn't pay enough to get anything but his men's contempt. Blair suspected these cowboys would gleefully blab the whole story as quickly as they could get to town. Blair looked at them and jerked his chin toward the corrals. "Them's your boss' cows in there. Go drive them back where they belong."

The two rode over to the dusty corral and swung the wire gate open. One went in and pushed the bawling cattle out while the other waited beyond the gate to get them started in the right direction. Blair Bishop swung stiffly onto his big gray horse and stood ready to see that none of the cattle cut back or ran off. They were of a common strain, mostly Longhorn, a kind progressive ranchmen were trying to breed up and get rid of. He spotted a leggy, lanky C Bar bull in the bunch. That was one reason he hated so badly to see Cass' cattle come over here, apart from the fact that he was short of grass and water himself. Bishop's place was under fence now, and he was buying better bulls to upgrade his herd. Every time a C Bar bull came over, it meant some of Blair's cows were going to fetch up a scrubby calf.

Somehow Clarence Cass got his voice back and his courage up. "You're a greedy man, Blair Bishop. You're a selfish man and no neighbor at all."

Cass' opinion of Blair was of no concern except as a matter of idle curiosity. "How do you figure that, Clarence?"

"Anybody can tell you've had all the luck. It rained more on you than it did on me. You made more grass than I did. I don't expect the Lord really intended to favor you over me; He'd of wanted you to share."

"We both had the same rain, Clarence, and that was mighty little. Difference is, you abused your land. Now you're payin' for it. Let's don't bring the Lord in on the argument."

A little distance away, Allan Bishop sat on his horse near Jessie Cass. They weren't talking; Jessie was looking shamefacedly at the ground.

Clarence Cass said harshly, "Well, if you ain't sharin', then I ain't."

"What do you mean by that?"

"That boy of yours, he ain't goin' to have nothin' from my little girl. You tell him that. You tell him if he don't leave my little Jessie alone, I'll fill his britches with buckshot."

"Don't look to me like she wants to be left alone."

"You just tell him, Blair Bishop. I wouldn't have her marryin' into no family that won't help a neighbor."

"Marry?" Blair was startled. That was the first time the thought of marriage had occurred to him. "Hell no, I wouldn't have it either. If my boy was to pull a stunt like that, I wouldn't let him *or* her back on the place."

Cass glared. "You don't think a Cass is good enough for your boy?"

"I sure as hell don't. Now, your cows are on their way, Clarence. I'd be much obliged if you'd go with them. And take your girl."

Cass started to ride off but paused for a last word. "Someday you'll be wishin' you had a good neighbor."

"I been wishin' that for years."

III

Blair Bishop sat there awhile, watching the cattle move slowly toward Cass country, the heavy dust clouding them over and hiding them much of the time. He pitied the cattle, because he knew they would find little to eat where they were going. But if he let them stay here, they would simply starve themselves and his own as well, for if Clarence Cass got by with a hundred, he would push in a hundred more. There was no bottom to the man's shabby greed.

Hez Northcutt said, "Want me to trail along and see that they all get there, Mister Bishop?"

"Yes, Hez. And take Allan with you."

Hez looked away. "Allan's gone. Rode off toward the house."

Irritated, Blair said, "All right, go ahead. Stay behind them and don't get into no trouble. Just let them know you're back there watchin' them. That'll be enough."

He turned toward the foreman, black-moustached Finn Goforth. "Finn, you and me, we'd just as well go in."

Ahead of him a long way, he could see Allan riding alone, nursing his anger.

Marry! Blair clenched his big aching fist. Sure, that Jessie was a fetching-looking girl. He had wondered sometimes if Clarence was really her father or if perhaps her mother had had a secret. Jessie was better looking than what a boy was apt to find down on Silky Row in Two Forks. But to be foolish enough to marry her! Maybe he had been giving Allan too much benefit of the doubt.

Blair Bishop had always been a summer man. Cold weather had a way of creeping into his bones, but give him hot weather and he was in his element. The sweat broke free and easy, and it seemed to take out some of the rheumatism with it. He enjoyed the touch of the hot west wind against his face, cooling him as it reached through his sweat-streaked shirt. Pride always welled up in him when he rode along letting his gaze reach from north to south, east to west, knowing that everything he could see from here was his. Droughty though it was, he had earned every foot of it, and he wouldn't ever want to give it up to anyone but the sons for whom he and Elizabeth had struggled so long. Blair had taken trail-drive money to buy the first of his holdings a long time ago, leasing state and school land to go with it. In later years, as school lands went up for claiming, he had gotten his cowboys to homestead claims. They proved them up for the required three years. Then, if they didn't want to keep the land, they sold it to Blair for a profit. A few had kept, but most had sold. Gradually the Blair Bishop ranch had grown. And with it Blair Bishop had grown too, certain he had the world by the tail on a downhill pull.

What he hadn't counted on was running out of water. The whole south end of his place was dry. In a dozen places he had dug wells in hopes of finding underground water, but it wasn't there. He found only caliche and dry sand. On the south half of the place he depended upon dug surface tanks to catch and hold runoff water when it rained. Now all these tanks were dry but one. The cattle on his entire south ranch depended upon water from one place — the Black Bull Tank.

If he could just get through this drought, Blair had sworn, he wouldn't be caught in this kind of trap again. He was going to have a lot more good tanks to catch and hold water. He would never again have all his chips riding on the Black Bull Tank.

He jerked his thumb to the right. "Let's go by and see how that new tank is comin', Finn."

They could see the dust before they saw the tank site. Blair heard the scrape of metal against hard-packed earth. A black dog came barking to meet them. A man shouted lustily, and a pair of mules trudged out onto a mound of fresh-turned earth, pulling a long-handled fresno loaded with dirt. A man in overalls jerked up the handle, flipping the fresno forward to dump its load upon the mound, the dust swirling about him. The mules moved quicker, relieved of the heavy burden. The man shouted at them again, pulling the lines and turning them back down into a broad basin he was laboriously hollowing out of the ground. He didn't see the horsemen until they rode up on the mound. He pulled the mules to a halt and wrapped the lines around the fresno handle. He stepped forward, taking off his hat and wiping sweat onto a dirt-crusted handkerchief he had used too many times already.

"Evenin', Mister Bishop. Evenin', Finn."

Blair Bishop nodded. "You're comin' along fine with it, Joe. That tank'll catch a right smart of water if it ever decides to rain again."

Joe Little shook his head. "A right smart. But it don't look much like rain today. I may be able to build a dozen more like this before we ever see a drop."

"I hope not. I wouldn't have nothin' left to pay you with, nor no cattle to drink out of it."

A boy walked across the basin carrying a jug wrapped in a wet towsack to keep its contents cool. "You need a drink of water, Joe? Howdy, Finn. Howdy, Dad."

Blair looked at him without surprise. "Billy, I thought I sent you to the south line camp with a wagonload of supplies."

"I already been. On my way back I thought I'd stop and help Joe awhile."

Billy looked a lot like Allan, except he was several years younger and not yet as big. One thing about it, Clarence Cass didn't have any daughters Billy's size, so maybe that was one worry Blair wouldn't have to put up with as Billy got older.

When the water jug had been passed around, Blair swung down and stiffly dropped to one knee to feel the earth in the bottom of the basin. "You reckon this one'll hold water, Joe?"

"There's caliche under it, but I ain't got it

scooped down to that depth yet. I think it'll be all right."

"I sure hope so. If there's one thing this drought has taught me, it's that it's as bad to run out of water as to run out of grass. This country tends to be shy of both."

Joe Little nodded. He was a small man with a grin as bright as all sunup, his teeth shining through thick brown dust and three weeks' growth of whiskers. "Me and my mules, we can't make it rain, Mister Bishop. But if it does rain, we can sure see to it that you're fixed to catch water."

"Fine, Joe. We'll be gettin' in. You comin', Billy?"

Billy Bishop shook his head. "I'll be in for supper. I still got time to spell Joe with his mules an hour or so first."

One thing about Blair's boys, Allan and Billy both . . . they weren't afraid of work. In Billy's case it wasn't so much that he liked building tanks as it was that he liked being around Joe Little. Joe had more good stories than a man could listen to in a year. Blair always figured he made most of them up as he went along, which was harmless enough if the listener realized that and didn't take them for more than they were worth. Billy needed to learn sooner or later that not everything he was told in this world was Bible-sworn truth.

Finn Goforth glanced back over his shoulder, watching Billy take over the fresno and bring it across the basin for a fresh, deep bite of earth. "Mister Bishop, you sure Joe Little is a good influence on that boy?"

"What do you mean?"

"Him bein' a reformed bank robber and all. At least, I hope he's reformed."

"He ain't given me no reason to doubt him. He works like hell."

"He's got reason to owe you. You was the only one around here would give him a job after he come home from the pen. But that don't mean he might not take a notion someday to try it all over again. It'd be a bad experience for Billy."

Blair shrugged. "I don't think Joe would ever do that, not anymore. Anyway, a boy's got to learn for himself that it's not all rosy the way they write it in books. He's got to learn that people will lie to you, steal from you, cheat you . . . maybe even kill you. I don't think he'll learn that from Joe, except maybe the lyin' part, and Joe's lies don't mean any harm."

When they reached the barn at headquarters, Blair found Allan sitting in the shade of the building patching a stirrup leather. Blair unsaddled his big gray and watched a moment as the animal rolled in the dust, ridding itself of the saddle's itch. Blair walked into the barn and flung his saddle up onto its place on the rack, hooked the bridle over the horn and dropped the wet blanket over it all. He walked back out and stood a moment in silence, waiting for Allan to say something. Allan didn't look at him.

"Son, I'll ask Chaco to get supper fixed a little early. I'm hungry as a wolf."

Allan only glanced at him, then went back to his work. "I'll eat at the bunkhouse with the boys tonight," he said tightly.

Blair rubbed his stiff, aching right hand. "Boy, what we done today, we done out of necessity. I told you. You know that old man."

"You don't have to tell me anything about Clarence Cass."

"What goes for him goes for his kin."

Allan looked his father in the eye. "I'll agree with everything you say about Clarence. But you don't know nothin' at all about Jessie."

"Know the bull, and you know the calf." Blair turned slowly, his hip hurting a little, giving him a slight limp as he strode toward the white frame house with the tall narrow windows that he had built for Elizabeth after so many years of dugouts and picket shacks. She hadn't lived long enough to see the first coat of paint start to peel.

He saw a man sitting on the front gallery, and he paused a moment to squint. Blair couldn't recognize him at the distance, but he didn't quicken his pace. He had found long ago that good news would keep, and bad news didn't get any better for rushing it. This could be a cattle buyer, which would be good news, or it could be the tax collector.

He found it was neither. "Howdy, Erly," Blair said as he mounted the steps. "How's the high sheriff?"

Erly Greenwood had pushed up from the rawhide-bottomed straight chair and stood at the top of the steps, hand outstretched. "Evenin', Blair. How's yourself?"

"Younger than ever, except for a little rheumatism. You ain't reached that stage in life yet." He studied the sheriff with pleasure. "You're lookin' good, Erly. That Alice must be feedin' you well. Been a long time since you been out our way. This calls for a drink." He pushed open the carved front door with its oval glass and shouted, "Chaco, bring us a bottle out here."

Chaco Martinez fetched it. Blair offered it to Erly, but the sheriff motioned for Blair to take first drink. Blair did. He sighed in pleasure, wiping his sleeve across his mouth. "Some things fade as the years go by. Others just get better. Good whiskey and good friends, that's two things that always pleasure a man." He watched Erly tilt the bottle, then dropped his dirty hat on the floor and settled into the rocking chair he kept on the gallery for enjoying the evening breeze. "Chaco'll have supper ready directly. Looks like if you don't stay the night, I'm liable to have to eat by myself."

"I'll stay. I'd be half the night gettin' back to town."

Blair noticed that the warmth faded from the sheriff's face, and a worried frown replaced it. Blair considered. No, it wasn't election year; something else must be eating on him. Blair said, "We miss you out here, Erly. I've got good help, mind you, but I don't reckon there's ever been a better cowboy on this place than you was. Before you started puttin' on weight, that is."

Erly nodded. "I suppose I was a fair to middlin' hand. Times, I wish I was cowboyin' again. Seemed like then I always knew what to do."

"And now you don't?"

Erly shook his head. "Right now I'm in the water up to my neck, and it's still risin'.

I got to tell an old friend some bad news, and I also got to tell him there's not a damn thing I can do."

"You talkin' about me, Erly?"

"You, Blair. I come to tell you Macy Modock is back."

Blair Bishop stopped rocking the chair. He sat in silence a minute or two, remembering, oblivious to the rising breeze riffling his thick gray hair. "You seen him, Erly?"

"Seen him and talked to him. Acts like he's back to stay." While Blair chewed his lip, the sheriff said, "I told him to keep right on movin', but I got no authority to make him do it. He's out free and legal. Long's I don't catch him breakin' the law, there's not a thing I can do about him, accordin' to the statutes." He paused. "There's a thing or two I could do *outside* of the statutes. With a man like Modock, I don't think there's many would criticize me."

"What could you do?"

"A man with his record, it'd be easy to trump up somethin' on him."

"You wouldn't want to do that, Erly."

"But I'd do it if you asked me to."

Blair Bishop passed the bottle to him again. "You know I wouldn't ask you. I wouldn't want you to."

"I didn't figure you would. So that leaves

Modock sittin' there and us sittin' here, wonderin' what he's got on his mind."

"He didn't give you no idea?"

"Blair, he swore ten years ago that you'd pay for havin' him put away. He had a real good system goin' for him . . . a busy saloon, a cattle-runnin' business, even a little bit of bank robbery on the side. Hadn't been for you, I never could've nailed him. It was you that hired the special prosecutor and run all his sidekicks out of the country so the jury could get up courage to convict him."

"There's not much he could do except come right out and kill me. I doubt that he cares to hang."

"He wouldn't of come back here if he didn't have somethin' on his mind. He's still got a little money, Blair. It's been settin' in a bank drawin' interest all the time he's been gone. He could go someplace he wasn't known and set himself up decent. But he's come back here."

Blair Bishop scowled, remembering how it had been before Macy Modock was sent away. "So it leaves us out on the end of the limb."

"And Macy Modock with a saw in his hand."

Blair looked at the bottle, decided he didn't want another drink and offered it to

Erly. The sheriff shook his head. Blair said, "Well, I don't intend to sit here and sweat, wonderin' about him. I'll go back to town with you in the mornin'. I'll talk to him myself."

The sheriff fretted. "I don't know if that's a good idea. It might come to a shootin'."

"Not if I don't take a gun with me." He held up his rheumatic right hand. "Look at that. Most times I can't even hold a pistol anymore, much less shoot one."

"It puts you at a bad disadvantage, Blair."

"But it puts him there too. He can't shoot a man that ain't got a gun and couldn't use one if he had it. He didn't come out after ten years in the pen rarin' to go right back."

They dismissed Macy Modock from conversation, but he remained on both their minds during the long periods of silence between the subjects they drummed up to talk about. Billy Bishop came home finally, face and clothes covered with dust from the tank-building job. Chaco Martinez met him at the gallery and made him strip off the clothes right there and walk around back to wash before he came into the house. That, Blair thought, was what Elizabeth would have done had she lived. Chaco, cranky but competent, was no substitute for a wife and mother, though without him Blair didn't know how he would have managed the house and the care of two boys.

Blair kept looking for Allan to come up from the bunkhouse, but his older son never showed. Finally he said to Billy, "Why don't you go tell your brother it's time for him to go to bed?"

Billy Bishop avoided his father's eyes. "He's not here, Dad." Pressed, he added, "He was saddlin' up a horse when I came in. Said he had an errand to run. I don't figure you sent him on any errand, Dad."

Blair shook his head, for both he and Billy knew where Allan had gone. Billy held his silence awhile, then put in, "Dad, maybe you ought to get to know Jessie better. Maybe she's not as bad as you think."

"I'm not sayin' she's bad, son. I'm just sayin' she was foaled in a poor stable."

There never was a time that Blair Bishop could walk into this house without Elizabeth crossing his mind. Times like this he missed her most of all. Maybe a mother could have talked to a son in a way a father couldn't.

IV

He was up before daylight next morning.
He met his sons and Erly Greenwood in the
kitchen, where Chaco Martinez was frying
up steak for breakfast, humming a Mexican
song about the dark ties between love and
death. Blair hadn't slept much, and he
guessed his face showed it. He fastened his
gaze on Allan. "Son, you went someplace
last night."

"Yes, sir, I did."

"You know I don't want you goin' there
no more."

"Dad, I've never argued with you. I don't
intend to. So that's one subject I just don't
want to talk to you about."

"We *will* talk about it."

"*You* can. I'm not goin' to listen." Allan
got up and started toward the door. Blair
waited until Allan had his hand on the
doorknob. He called, "Come on back, boy,
and eat your breakfast. We'll talk about it

another time."

Blair Bishop hadn't lost many battles in his life. He had an uneasy feeling he was going to lose this one. Sure, he could do one thing; he could flat forbid Allan ever to go to the Cass place again. And likely as not Allan would pack up and leave the ranch, then do what he damn well pleased. That, Blair knew, was what *he* would have done if the same situation had occurred twenty-five or thirty years ago. But of course it hadn't. Elizabeth had been one thing. A daughter of Clarence Cass was another.

The sheriff had not mentioned Macy Modock to Blair's sons or to Chaco, who would quickly blab it. Blair made a point to say nothing. Time enough for that after he had a chance to meet Modock face to face.

He sensed that people were watching him as he rode into Two Forks with Erly Greenwood. The word about Modock must have gotten around by now. Those people who had lived here ten years ago wouldn't have any trouble remembering. The rest had no doubt heard enough. He rode through town, tying up beside Erly at a hitchrack in front of the courthouse. The hostler from the Two Forks Livery & Grain came shuffling toward them as fast as he could move without breaking into a trot.

41

"Mornin', Mister Bishop. Reckon Erly's told you?"

Blair nodded. "He told me."

"It was me that seen Macy first, Mister Bishop. I knowed he meant trouble, and I went straight to the sheriff. I knowed that was what you'd of wanted me to do, and I done it."

Blair decided Harley Mills was casting around for some kind of reward. He also knew that anything he gave Harley would wind up being spent or traded for whiskey. Blair had given Harley a good chance once and had seen him drink it up. Blair Bishop was not much given to second chances. "Thanks, Harley. Where's Macy at?"

"A little while ago he was settin' in the Bar & Billiard Emporium. Had a redheaded feller with him. They come to town together. They both got guns on." The hostler had glanced at Blair's hip and saw no pistol there. He began to realize Blair didn't intend to give him anything, and he showed his disappointment.

"All right, Harley." Blair couldn't tell whether Harley was concerned about him or just wanting to be sure he saw the whole show. He suspected the latter. He looked a moment toward the saloon, dreading.

"Well, Erly, I guess this is what I come for."

"I'm goin' with you."

"No, you're not. I told you, you bein' there with a gun — or even that badge — might trigger somethin' off."

"What if he shoots you, Blair?"

Blair Bishop came close to making a dry smile. "Then I reckon you can come on over."

The ride into town had stiffened Blair's legs, and he walked slowly, that cursed limp plaguing him. Damn it, why couldn't a man go into his autumn years with a little dignity? His mouth went dry as he neared the building. Blair Bishop had never feared any man, and he didn't fear Macy Modock. But he disliked trouble and would ride around it when he could. Whether this meeting meant trouble or not, he knew it was a cinch to be unpleasant. He'd already had enough unpleasantness to do him for a lifetime.

The heavy bartender stepped out the front door and moved to meet him. His long moustaches drooped, and his bushy eyebrows were knitted in concern. "Mister Bishop, you know who's in there?"

Blair nodded. "I know."

"You and me been friends a long time, Mister Bishop. I don't want nothin' hap-

43

penin' to you in my bar."

"Nothin's fixin' to happen. I'm goin' to talk to him, is all."

"He's been settin' there like he was waitin' for somethin'. You, maybe. I don't like the feel of it."

"If he's waitin' for me, there's no use me puttin' things off."

"You ain't packin' no gun, Mister Bishop, but he is. And so's that mean-eyed one he's got with him. They could kill you in a second."

"That's how come I left my gun at home. There won't be no trouble."

The bartender glanced at the door. "All right, Mister Bishop. But I got my shotgun behind the bar, loaded and cocked. If that Modock makes one bad move, I'll let him have both barrels."

Blair nodded his thanks. He stepped up onto the little wooden porch and through the open door. He sensed the bartender coming in behind him and moving to his place behind the bar. Blair Bishop blinked, then saw three men seated at a little table. He gave the red-bearded one a brief glance and pegged him for a gunfighter. That cinched it; Modock hadn't come here looking for sunshine and pretty songs. He turned to the tall, lanky man with the black

44

eyes and unlighted cigar.

"Macy. Been a long time."

"Ten years, two months and twenty-one days. I counted them every one."

It relieved Blair that Macy made no move to shake hands, for Blair had no intention of doing it. He noted that the ten years had been hard on Macy Modock. The man seemed to have aged twenty since he had left here. He was thinner, his cheeks sunken in, his shoulders a little drooped. Macy's hair was shorter than he used to wear it . . . prison cut, Blair figured. And it was sprinkled with gray where once it had been coal black. But his eyes hadn't changed. They had always looked hard as steel. They were framed in darker circles now than ever before, and if anything, they were harder.

Modock motioned toward the red-bearded man. "This here is Owen Darby. We was partners, you might say, back in *school.* We worked on the same pile of rocks."

Blair nodded. That fit his first appraisal.

Modock motioned toward a thin, black-suited little man on the other side of him. "Bishop, you ain't yet said good mornin' to Judge Quincy."

Blair said, "I *never* say good mornin' to Judge Quincy."

The little man's lip turned down in an

angry scowl. In Bishop's view, Quincy was a cheap, scheming lawyer who made his living defending the indefensible and hunting for loopholes in the statutes. He had never been a judge in his life, and he never would be one unless the government went plumb to hell. Someone had hung the name on him as a cheap saloon joke, and it had stuck to him ever since. Folks said "Judge" with a bit of a snicker.

Modock said, "I'll grant you the judge didn't have much luck defendin' me, but then he was up against the best legal talent that a rich man's money could buy. He's had pretty good luck in some other cases, though. I count him as a friend."

Every man to his own kind, Blair thought. "I come to town because I figured you and me might have somethin' to talk about, Macy. Do we?"

"I don't know. What do you think?" Modock seemed to sense that he held all the cards. "Bothers you, don't it, me bein' here?"

"Like knowin' there's a rattlesnake under my porch and not bein' able to get at him. It bothers me that they ever let you out. It'd bother me knowin' you was anyplace, Macy, except in jail. But you're here, and I want to know what you're plannin' to do."

Modock took the cigar from his mouth, eyeing Blair Bishop levelly, his own eyes unreadable. "Can't say that I've made up my mind. If I do, maybe I'll let you know."

"If you got any notions about gettin' even with me, Macy, you better forget them. What I done to you, you had comin' in spades. I don't want trouble with you, but I won't stand still for no foolishness."

Macy dipped the end of his cigar in his whiskey glass, soaked it a moment, then shoved it back into his mouth. "Now, what do you think I might do to you, Bishop? You was a big man before, and you're bigger now. Got you a fine ranch, lots of cattle. And me, what have I got to show for all that time? Ten years cut out of my life, cut out of me the way you'd rip the guts out of a catfish."

"You've still got a little money, Macy, from what I hear. And you still got time. You could do a right smart for yourself if you was of a mind to."

Macy grinned, his teeth clamped on the cold cigar. "And I will, Bishop; you can just bet I will."

Blair felt his hackles rise. "You'd do better someplace else. Take your money and go where they don't know you."

"But I couldn't collect what's owed me if

I was to go someplace else. And I'm figurin' on collectin', Bishop. From you, most of all." He used the cigar as a pointer, jabbing it toward Blair. "I had ten years to study about you, and believe me I done a lot of thinkin'. For a long time if I'd of had the chance, I'd of just come back and shot you dead wherever I found you. But gradually it come to me that there's better ways of killin' a man than shootin' him. There's ways to kill him off an inch at a time till there's nothin' left of him but a little dab of cold sweat. I decided that's what I'd do to you, Bishop, just whittle away at you.

"I see you ain't wearin' a gun. Probably haven't in years. But before I'm done, you'll wear one. Maybe in the end you'll get so desperate you'll come gunnin' after me and I can finish the job nice and legal, in self-defense."

Color surged into Bishop's face. His arthritic right hand convulsed. There had been a time if anyone had talked to him like that he would have shot him on the spot. But that had been a long time ago, before the years mellowed him, and before an accumulation of old pains and injuries half crippled him. He said quietly, "I'm sorry it's this way, Macy. I expected it would be, but I'm sorry just the same." He turned, his big Mexican spurs jingling as he limped heavily across the pine floor and out onto the porch. A strong dread rose up in him, and a helplessness.

He walked across the street to where the sheriff waited beside the tied horses. Bishop didn't speak, so Erly Greenwood did.

"Talkin' to him didn't help, did it?"

Bishop shook his head. "The hate's as strong as it ever was."

The sheriff suggested, "What I told you yesterday still goes. Just say the word and I'll trump up somethin'."

"It'd never set right with you, Erly, or with me. No, we'll just wait, and we'll hope. Sooner or later he'll make a mistake."

"By that time," said Greenwood, "you could be dead."

Modock got up from his chair and walked to the door to watch Blair Bishop limp across the street. He saw him in conversation with the sheriff. Modock chewed the cigar savagely, his hard eyes glittering with the pent-up hatred of ten hellish years.

The red-whiskered Owen Darby spat at a brass bowl and missed. "You got your stomach churnin', Macy. I can hear it from where I sit. If I hated a man that much, I'd just shoot him and be done with it."

Modock glanced around at the heavy bartender and decided to ignore him. He didn't give a damn what a bartender thought. "Did you ever get so hungry for somethin', Owen, that when you finally got it you ate it slow and spaced it out to make it last as long as you could?" When Darby shook his head, Modock said, "No, I expect you never did, so you can't begin to understand. *You* kill a man quick, the way a wolf does. If it's a man like Bishop, I'd rather do it slow and play with him awhile, like a cat."

A young woman walked by in the street. From the scarlet hue of her crinolines, Modock surmised she might come from down on Silky Row. "Talk about hungry . . . a man don't know how long ten years can be when he never feels the touch of a woman, never hears the laugh in a woman's voice. That's somethin' else Blair Bishop owes me for . . . ten years without a woman." He glanced at the bartender. "Things still alive on Silky Row, the way they used to be?"

The bartender made no attempt to hide his dislike. "Just about. But I doubt *you're* as alive as you used to be."

Modock grunted and walked back to the table. He stared at the little lawyer. "Judge, how long you think it'll take you to go through all them deeds of Bishop's?"

Quincy sat rigid, ill at ease in the company of these two. "Some time. And it'll require some money too. A task like this is not undertaken lightly."

"You'll get your money; I promised you that. Find me the right flaws in them deeds and you'll get a lot *more* money." He leaned over the table. "Let me down and you'll eat every law book in your office, one at a time."

"Mister Modock, you have no right . . ."

Modock punched his finger into Quincy's breastbone hard enough to bring pain. "I don't give a damn about rights. You just do what I tell you!"

V

Joe Little put the can of tomatoes on the ground, opened the blade of his pocketknife and punched a hole through the tin. He punched a second at a right angle, the ends of the slits coming together in a V. He pushed the cut part down with his thumb and offered the can to Billy Bishop. Billy, trained to defer to his elders, shook his head. "You first."

Little tilted the can up and took a long swallow. He passed it over to Billy. "Boy," he said, "you got to quit bringin' me stuff like this out of your old daddy's pantry. He's furnishin' me grub enough."

"Not tomatoes or peaches or stuff like that. Anyway, he can afford a can of somethin' now and then."

"I don't know. If it don't rain pretty soon, he might not be able to buy nothin'. You got to quit it, Billy. That's stealin'."

"It's not stealin' when you take it out of

your own house. That's not like stealin' cattle, or takin' from a bank, or . . ." He broke off short, realizing he was edging into deep water. "Anyway, Dad knows about it. He's seen me. And you deserve somethin' special once in a while. This is hard work, buildin' tanks."

Joe Little studied the can awhile in silence. "Did I ever tell you, boy, about the time I shared a can of tomatoes with John Wesley Hardin?"

Billy smiled. "Just happens you did. Only, the last time you said it was Billy the Kid."

Joe Little frowned. "I believe you're right. It *was* Billy the Kid. What I shared with Wes Hardin was a pot of coffee."

Joe's black dog set in to barking and trotted across the newly dug basin. Joe stood up to look. He almost dropped the can. He said something under his breath, his eyes going wide.

Billy jumped to his feet. "What is it, Joe?" Joe didn't reply, so Billy looked for himself. A hundred yards away came two men on horseback. They were strangers to Billy.

Joe said: "If I didn't know better, I'd swear that was Macy Modock, but he's in jail."

Billy shook his head. "No, he's out. You hadn't heard?"

"I ain't heard nothin' but a hooty owl and

you in a month of Sundays."

"They been talkin' a little around the ranch. They don't say much that I can hear. I remember there was hard feelin's once between him and Dad. Is he back to make trouble, Joe?"

"I don't know, boy." Joe Little shook his head. "Anywhere he's at, he's goin' to make trouble." He sagged a bit.

Billy looked at him in surprise. "You know Macy Modock?"

"I know him, boy. I've stretched the truth a mite about some of them other fellers, but I sure as hell know Macy Modock. We was . . . in *school* together. Shared a room awhile, so to speak."

"You mean you was cellmates?"

Joe Little dropped any pretense. "We was cellmates. For me, it was like bein' denned up with a rattler."

Macy Modock and Owen Darby eased their horses down into the basin and rode across to where Little and Billy stood on the fresh-made dump. Modock lifted his hand and made a dim sort of smile. "Howdy, Joe. Folks in town told me you was workin' out here."

Joe looked at first one man, then the other, worry creasing his dust-powdered face. "Folks in town talk too much. How do, Macy, Darby . . ." There was no greeting in his voice. The black dog sniffed suspiciously around the strange horses and backed off, as if deciding that if his master didn't like the company, he didn't either. He barked again from a careful distance.

Macy Modock stared at Billy. "I'd judge by the looks that this boy would be a Bishop. Howdy, boy."

Billy Bishop had been raised to be civil right up to the moment he swung his fist. "How do, Mister Modock."

Modock's attention stayed with Billy. "I swear, he sure does favor his old daddy. I bet that old man sets a heap of store in you, don't he, boy?"

Joe Little took that for an implied threat. "Macy, this boy is a friend of mine. You leave him alone."

"I'm a friend of yours too, Joe."

"That all depends, Macy. It all depends."

Modock watched the boy a minute longer, then said, "Button, I got somethin' to discuss with my old friend Joe Little. Don't you reckon you could find you somethin' to do while we talk? Go work them mules and that fresno, maybe."

Billy looked uncertainly at Joe. Joe silently motioned with his chin for him to go ahead. Reluctantly Billy walked down into the basin where the mules waited patiently, in no hurry to work again. Joe Little moved off of the dump on the side away from the wind so the dust wouldn't reach him. Modock and Owen Darby followed him a-horseback. Joe turned and said curtly, "You said you wanted to talk. I don't see we got anything to talk about, but go ahead."

"Maybe we *ain't* got anything to talk about, but I thought I'd come see for myself if it was true what I heard . . . that Joe Little was sweatin' hisself into the ground for Blair Bishop."

"I'm bein' paid a fair wage. I got over two hundred dollars in the bank. That's more money than I ever had in my life before . . . legally."

"Two hundred dollars? Why, friend, you made that much money once in an hour."

"I said legally."

"If I remember right, Blair Bishop helped put you away, same as he done me."

"I had it comin'. I been ashamed ever since for what I done."

Modock's eyes narrowed. "Joe, I thought you had more in you. That black dog of yours yonder . . . if a man was to take a double of a rope to him, he'd tuck his tail between his legs and run. And it looks to

56

me like that's just what you done too. You've tucked your tail."

"I'm doin' honest work and earnin' an honest dollar."

"Workin' for a man who helped send you to jail. A man who probably despises you and'd tell you so if he didn't need you to bend your back for him."

Fear began to touch Joe Little, because he knew this pair was up to something, and he sensed they had a place in it for him. Otherwise they wouldn't have come out here. Macy Modock was not a man to waste his time on people he couldn't use. "Macy, if you got any notions that include me, forget it. I'm stayin' right where I'm at."

"Followin' a plow or a fresno, lookin' a pair of mules in the rump all day? I thought you had more ambition."

"I have. Someday it'll be my own mules, my own place."

"But still mules. You're a damn fool, Joe Little. I'm sorry we wasted our time."

"I'm sorry too. I'd of been happier if I'd never laid eyes on you again the rest of my life."

Anger came into Modock's dark-circled eyes. "Next time you're kissin' Blair Bishop's boots, remember we offered you a chance to get out. Goodbye, Joe. We'll see you in hell."

"Keep a place warm for me. You'll probably get there before I do."

Macy Modock drew rein and took a long look down toward the headquarters of the Clarence Cass place. "That's a greasy-sack outfit if ever I seen one," he muttered to Owen Darby. "A man can't have no pride to live in a place like that when he could do better." The house was small and plain, evidently put up by somebody who didn't know much about carpentering and didn't learn much on the job. It showed no evidence that it had ever known paint. The corrals were of brush, mostly, some of the fences leaning. One wild bull could have torn the whole thing out by the roots.

"Fits the rest of his country," Darby put in. "Whole place looks like it'd been sheeped into the ground."

"Not sheep," Modock said. "Just too many cattle. Dry weather come, the place couldn't feed them all."

A thin, sharp-hipped Longhorn steer eyed the riders warily and clattered off into a motte of live oaks, his tail high. He looked weak enough to fall if he tried to run very hard. Modock scowled. "I remember this place the way it used to be. Cass didn't have it then. We stole some pretty good cows off of the old boy who did."

"How come he left?"

"Went broke. They split up his country and sold it off to people like this Cass."

"Maybe you helped break him."

"Maybe. It was his lookout, not mine. It's every man's place to take care of hisself. If he can't do it, he ain't got no sympathy comin'." Modock took a long sweeping look over the land. "If it'd rain some, I could make a good place out of this, Owen . . . if it was mine. And maybe before we're through, it'll *be* mine."

They rode up to the barn first, where Modock saw a man lounging in the shade, a rawhide chair tilted against the wall. It seemed to Modock that the wall might have had a little lean to it, but he wasn't sure. He wouldn't be surprised, judging by the rest of the outfit. He spotted another man asleep farther out, under a wooden water tank that stood on a platform beside a cypress-vaned windmill. "Evenin'. We're lookin' for Clarence Cass."

The cowboy jerked awake, pushing the hat back out of his face and blinking sleepily. Modock had to repeat. The cowboy pointed. "He's up at the house. Clarence, he usually takes him a little nap in the heat of the day."

That didn't surprise Modock either. From the looks of the place, he would judge that nap ran from noon till about sundown.

Owen Darby said, "If you *was* to take over this place, I don't know what you'd want with it."

"It could be fixed up. Needs some changes made. Them lazy cowboys is the first thing I'd get rid of."

Riding toward the small house, Modock caught a quick glimpse of a young woman out back, hanging clothes on a sagging wire. He glanced at Darby in surprise. Nobody had mentioned to him about a girl out here. He turned back for a second look at her, but she had disappeared quickly into the house. "Owen," he said quietly, "place already looks better."

He swung down and looped his leather reins over a fence picket. Darby took his time, following behind as Modock strode up to the house, narrowed eyes sweeping everything in sight. The door was wide open, but Modock thought it best to observe the amenities, for now. He knocked on the door frame.

From inside, he could hear the woman's voice, speaking low, and he could hear a sleepy, confused grumbling. Broke up the old man's nap, he knew. Presently Clarence

Cass trudged to the door, trying to shove his shirttail into his waistband without bothering to unbutton his britches. He blinked at Modock without recognition. "You-all lookin' for somebody?"

Modock spoke with what pleasantness he was able to muster. "Yes, sir, we're lookin' for Clarence Cass, the owner of this place. You'd be him, I judge."

"Yes, sir, reckon I would."

"We'd be right favored if we could have a drink of cool water out of your cistern, sir. Then we'd like to talk some business with you."

"With me?" Cass, not completely over his nap, blinked uncertainly. "Sure, the cistern's right yonder. You-all cattle buyers?"

"No, sir."

"Then what business you got with me?"

Modock walked over to the cistern and turned the handle to lower the bucket into the well. He cranked it up again, conscious that Cass was waking rapidly now, and trailing him in his socks. He took his time about drinking the water, then passing it on to Darby, letting the old man's curiosity build. Cass repeated, "What's this business you was talkin' about?"

Modock turned to face him and motioned that they ought to go over and sit down in the shade. It was Cass' place, but already Modock was beginning to call the turn. "Mister Cass, I understand you had some difficulty the other day with Blair Bishop."

Cass for a moment eyed him with suspicion. "I'd say that was my business. Anyway, I ain't finished with Blair Bishop yet."

Modock nodded. "That's why we came. I'm Macy Modock. This here is my friend Owen Darby."

Realization came, and Cass' mouth went open. "Modock! Didn't know you was anywheres around. I've heard about you."

"Mostly lies, I expect, sir. There was a time I had a standin' in Two Forks . . . in this whole country. It was taken away from me by schemers and liars. Oh, I'll grant you, Mister Cass, I sure ain't no preacher. I expect when I get to the Pearly Gates, it'll take some talkin' to get me through. But I'm not near what some have painted me. Some like Blair Bishop . . ." He paused. "You should know, sir. I understand he's maligned you too."

Cass nodded vigorously. "One of these days my patience'll wear thin."

Modock reached into his pocket and took out a couple of cigars, handing one to Cass, biting into the other himself. "I thought maybe it already had. I thought you might be ready to do somethin' about it."

"I will. One of these days I damn sure will."

"It could be one day *soon,* if you was of a mind. Some folks in town, they told me you'd be a real good man for me to get together with. They said you was a man who knew what he wanted and wasn't afraid."

Cass' vanity was quickly touched. "Who was it said that?"

"Some folks." Modock took out a match but didn't light the cigar. He simply chewed it while his narrowed eyes studied Clarence Cass. Feeling he had lucked upon a sympathetic ear, Cass began to unburden himself of all the injuries he had suffered at the hands of the rich and overbearing Blair Bishop. Modock listened attentively, nodding every so often and speaking softly, "That's just the way it was done to me."

Owen Darby couldn't listen to it. Scowling, he walked off to poke around the place for himself.

At length Cass ran down, and Modock said, "I can tell you've got a just grievance, my friend. And I can tell that the folks in town was right. You're the man I been lookin' for."

Cass reached down and pulled up a saggy

sock. "What did you have in mind for me to do?"

"Just string along with me . . . back me up in whatever I say. We'll get even with Blair Bishop."

A sudden worry tugged in Cass' face. "But how? You ain't figurin' on killin' nobody, are you?"

"Killin'? The thought never once crossed my mind. I'd sooner scrub floors in the meanest dive in town than to kill somebody. No, what I got in mind will give us a chance to whittle Blair Bishop down, to break him piece by piece. You'll be in on it; you'll have the satisfaction. What's more, you'll have a chance to pick up some of the pieces when they fall. You'd like to have part of the Bishop ranch, wouldn't you, Mister Cass? You got a chance to get it."

"The Bishop ranch." A glow came into Cass' eyes, and he began rubbing his knuckles, enjoying the thought of it. "He's always lorded it over me, Blair Bishop has. He's got a better country, had better rain, always had all the luck when there's been others just as deservin' that the Almighty has passed by and left needful. It'd sure pleasure me . . ." He broke into a crooked grin. Modock guessed that was a sight few people had ever seen. Cass said, "I'm with you,

Mister Modock. What'll I do?"

"First off, you'll let it be known around that me and Owen, we're on a deal to buy in as partners with you."

Cass' eyebrows raised. "You ain't, are you?"

"Of course not. There won't be no papers signed. Later on you can say we backed out by mutual consent. But we need a base to operate from, a reason for some of the things I figure to do. You with us, friend?"

"*With* you, Mister Modock."

They shook hands, and Owen Darby came back. Modock said, "See there, Owen, I told you this was the man."

Clarence Cass straightened his bent shoulders and stood every bit of five and a half feet tall. "I'm proud you come, Macy. I never been one to brag; I always been one to keep my silence. Still waters runs the deepest, I've always thought."

"Truer words was never spoke, partner."

Cass turned toward the house and called: "Jessie! I want you to put a pot of coffee on for these men." The girl came hesitantly to the door. Modock stared, his dark eyes widening for a moment. She was seventeen, maybe eighteen, eyes blue, face slender and nice-featured, hair the soft brown of a good Morgan colt. And her figure . . . she was coming into the full bloom of womanhood. Modock kept staring, the pulse quickening in him. He'd visited down on Silky Row a little since he had been back in Two Forks, but that was tarnished merchandise. This, he sensed, was fresh goods, untried, unspoiled.

Cass introduced the girl to the two men. "Girl," he said, "Macy and Owen here, they're talkin' about goin' in as partners with us. I want you to fix them some coffee." He reconsidered. "No, by Godfrey, this calls for somethin' better than coffee. This calls for whiskey, and I got a new bottle still uncorked."

Modock took the bottle, but he didn't need it. The girl was enough for now, as long as he had been without. He watched her move about the house, and he decided. This ranch wasn't the only thing of Clarence Cass' that Macy Modock was going to have!

VI

In the darkness, Allan Bishop almost rode upon Joe Little's tank-building camp. He reined up sharply at the unexpected sight of Joe's mules hobbled on the short grass. The mules stirred in the pale moonlight, and in camp Joe Little called, "Who's out yonder?"

Allan's first impulse was to keep quiet and bluff it out, to make Joe think it was just a loose horse ambling by in the night. But he remembered Joe kept a shotgun in camp. He decided he'd be better off not finding out how good a shot Joe was.

"It's me, Joe. Allan Bishop."

"Allan!" Joe Little came out of the shallow basin where he had spread his bedroll. He wasn't carrying the shotgun. "Boy, you lost?"

Allan shook his head and dismounted. "I'd forgot you'd moved over here to start a new tank. If I'd thought, I'd of ridden way around and not bothered you."

"Your daddy decided he needed a second watering here close by the old Black Bull Tank. There's enough water gets down this draw sometimes to fill two tanks and leave plenty over." He eyed Allan suspiciously. "How come you out in the night thisaway?"

"Just ridin', Joe."

Little tilted his head. "Ain't but a mile or so yonder to old Clarence Cass' fence. That's where you're headin', ain't it?"

Allan nodded, uncomfortable.

"I'm not faultin' you, Allan. Ain't been many years since I was doin' the same. I know the way your pulse beats, but the way I heard it, Clarence said you wasn't to go over there no more, and Blair Bishop said the same thing."

"I'm of age, Joe. So's Jessie, pretty near." Allan's voice tightened in resentment. "Why don't they leave us alone, Joe? We're not hurtin' nobody. We got a right to lead our own lives."

"You're too young to understand it if I told you, and Blair Bishop's too old to understand your side of it. Maybe I'm at just the right age . . . halfway between. Your daddy thinks he's doin' what's best for you. As for old Clarence, he's a miserable little whelp, and deep down I expect he knows it. Your old daddy has shamed him. Clarence hasn't got the guts to lash out at Blair, but in his eyes you're still a button. His kind can always kick a dog or a kid."

"Sorry I bothered you, Joe. If anybody asks, you didn't see me."

"You watch out for that old man."

Allan rode away thinking he knew why his brother Billy liked to visit with Joe Little. Joe had been through the grinder. Joe understood.

It went against Allan Bishop's grain to go on the *cuidado,* to sneak around like a coyote. He had grown up watching his father meet everything and everybody head on, his shoulders square and his jaw set. He doubted that Blair Bishop had ever gone to a back door or followed the moonlight shadows in his life. They would probably bury Blair Bishop with his hat on.

But Allan found himself approaching Clarence Cass' place from the back side and stepping to the ground, tying his horse in the darkness of the mesquite brush a hundred yards from the barn. Allan paused in the edge of the shadow, looking around before he set out to cross the open strip that lay between him and the brush corrals. The house lay beyond, and so did a rough-lumber shed. Allan doubted he would be seen.

He waited a long time, wanting to roll a smoke but fearing the flare of the match might betray him. He leaned on the fence and stared at the lamplighted windows of the house. Presently he saw a quick movement, something passing between him and the light. In a moment a slender figure came around the corner of the corral and paused. A girl's voice reached him gentle and quiet. "Allan!"

"Over here, Jessie." He walked to meet her and swept her into his arms. He kissed her savagely, for the wanting was stronger now that they had been forbidden to each other. They said little at first, for all the love words had been spoken so many times before. At length, Allan said, "I've got a good mind to march up to the house and tell your old daddy I'm takin' you and he can go to hell!"

"What about your *own* daddy?"

"I'd tell him the same thing, if he pushed me."

"No you wouldn't. You respect him too much; you don't really want to hurt him. As for mine, I know what he is. But still, he's my father. So we'll wait."

"This business of meetin' in the dark, it's no good, Jessie. I feel like some kind of a criminal. I expect you do too."

70

"We got to do it this way or not see each other at all."

"We don't have to say nothing to either one of them, you know. We could just up and leave and not speak to anybody."

"It'd be the same thing, almost. Later on we'd be ashamed. We got a whole life to live together, Allan. We don't want to start it wrong."

"I don't know how long I can wait, Jessie. Seein' you this way, it sets me afire."

"Then maybe you better not be a-comin' over here again for a while."

"Not seein' you would be even worse."

She shook her head and buried her face against his chest.

"I don't know what the answer is, Allan. We just got to wait awhile. I don't know what my daddy would do for himself if I was to leave him."

"The whole place would come apart. If you hadn't worked like a span of mules, it'd already be gone. Sooner or later you got to leave him. He won't never be no readier for it than he is tonight."

"I'm afraid to leave him right now. Things are wrong out here. They been wrong ever since Macy Modock came."

"I hear he's bought into partnership."

"That's what he and Dad say. I haven't

seen any money change hands. There's somethin' wrong; I can't figure out just what. Dad hangs on him like a hound dog to a master, and yet I can tell that somehow Dad's afraid of him too. First thing Modock did was to fire our two cowhands. I could tell Dad didn't intend for him to do it, but Dad just stood there and didn't say a word. Modock's gradually takin' this place over. Dad's losin' his grip on it."

"I can't figure out what a man like Modock wants with a place like this. There's lots of better ones if he wanted to ranch."

"He's not a rancher. I don't know what he is exactly, but he's not a rancher. He scares me, Allan. He scares me to death."

"Has he done anything . . ."

She shook her head. "No. But did you ever get a sudden feelin' you was in danger, and then see a rattlesnake? An instinct, sort of. Times I get that feelin'. I look around, and there's Macy Modock watching me."

"All the more reason I ought to take you away from here."

"No, Allan, not for a while yet, anyway. If there's somethin' wrong, I don't want to leave my dad here by himself. We'll go when it's time. Till then we just got to wait."

She kissed him again. He caught her hands as she started to leave. He held them a moment, saw she meant what she had said, then reluctantly let her go. She turned once at the corner of the corral and looked back at him. Then she was gone.

Allan Bishop went to his horse.

In the shadows, Macy Modock stood watching the girl. He had followed her when she left the house with an excuse about seeing that the chickens were shut up. He had seen her take care of that chore before dark. Modock had stood back far enough that he could not make out the words, but he could hear the soft exchange of talk between boy and girl. He had trembled as he watched the girl move into Allan Bishop's arms. Watching her now as she walked slowly toward the house, it was all he could do to keep from striding after her, overtaking her, setting claim upon her and letting the fire in him run its course. But the slow fire of his hatred burned steadier, and it prevailed. There were other things to be done first.

He looked toward the brush where the young man had gone, and where hoofbeats trailed away in the night. It would be easy to ride after Allan Bishop, to kill him and fling his body upon Blair Bishop's porch. What better way to punish the man than by robbing him of his son?

But Modock knew that would cut vengeance short. That would put him on the run. Maybe he would have time to kill Blair Bishop, and maybe he wouldn't.

No, he would wait. All things would come to him in their own due course. He would kill Blair Bishop, but it would be in his own time, and under conditions of his own choosing.

VII

A full moon sent long shadows slanting out ahead of three riders. They moved in an easy trot across the rolling land, unshod hoofs raising dry dust to pinch the nostrils of horses and men. One man kept hanging back and looking nervously around him, twisting his skinny frame first one way, then the other.

"Macy, I oughtn't to be with you on this. If old Blair Bishop was to catch me on his country of a night, he'd turn me wrongside out. You know he's bound to miss them cattle sooner or later. You know who he'll suspicion first."

Macy Modock glanced at Owen Darby, then growled impatiently at Cass. "I wisht you'd quit your bellyachin', Clarence. I've listened to about all I'm goin' to. Hush up or I'll set you afoot, and then maybe he *will* catch you."

"Old Bishop . . . when he gets mad, he

don't fool around."

"Clarence . . ." Modock's voice carried threat.

But Clarence Cass had bottled up too much anxiety to quit talking.

"You got no right to make me come along with you on a thing like this. I ain't stole none of Bishop's cows, and I didn't want to be no part of what you're fixin' to do tonight."

Modock grunted savagely. "I figure as long as we're partners we ought to share everything, the risk as well as the spoils. You been grinnin' like a possum, watchin' the boys ride out of a night to haze off Bishop stock. It tickled you, long's you wasn't a part of it. Now I figure it's time you *became* a part of it. You'll be a better partner, Clarence, once you've got your own feet muddied a little, same as ours. You won't be as apt to change your mind about things, or go around talkin' when you ought to be a-listenin'. Now catch up and stay up!"

They reached the fence. Modock dismounted, took a pair of wire pinchers from his saddle and pulled out the staples that held the wire. He had to remove them from two posts to make the wires loose enough that he could press them to the ground and let the horses walk over onto the Double B side of the fence. Clarence Cass held back, and for a moment Modock thought he would have to go fetch him. But Cass came finally, complaining all the way.

"What'll we do if Bishop catches us?"

"What'd he be doin' out this time of the night? He's gettin' on in years. He needs his rest."

"I'm as old as he is. I need mine too," Cass whimpered, watching Modock put the staples back in place so the men's entry would not so easily be noticed. They would ride out this way again, but they might not hit the same place in the fence. "Besides, I don't like leavin' that little girl of mine there all by herself with them men of yours on the place. Can't ever tell what ideas'll come into the mind of men like that."

"You know damn well what kind of ideas they have. But I told them I'd put a bullet in the man that touches her. Besides, they got an errand of their own. They'll go out and pick up some more of them Double B cattle tonight."

"Bishop won't hold still when he finds out somebody's takin' his cows."

"He's got too many anyway, dry as it is. Besides, he can't tie it to me and you, Clarence. He won't find no tracks leadin' to our place."

Cass winced. "Our place? It's still my place."

Modock nodded. "I find that awful easy to forget." He rode in silence awhile, then asked, "You sure we're headed in the right direction for that tank?"

Cass' shoulders were slumped in resignation. "I told you. The Black Bull Tank lies yonderway. It ain't fair, really. It sets on a draw leadin' out of my country. Old Bishop catches the water that runs off of my place, and he won't share none of it."

"You could build a tank of your own and stop most of the runoff."

"I will one of these days. Just never have had the time."

Modock spat, his contempt bubbling close to the surface. "You sure this tank has got a weak bottom in it?"

"I'm sure. Harley Mills cowboyed for him a few years. He told me how much trouble they had at first, makin' it hold water. It kept seepin' down through the bottom. Finally they brought all the Double B horses over here and held them in the tank bottom half a day, millin' them around so their hoofs would pack the ground. Nothin' packs like a remuda of horses."

"If we crack that tight bottom, won't take long for the water to seep right on through.

Give it a few days and Bishop's Black Bull Tank will be nothin' but a black *mud* tank."

A dog barked, and Macy Modock hauled up on his reins. "What's a dog doin' way out here in the far side of a pasture?"

Cass shrugged. "Stray."

Modock listened, suspicious. "You sure you ain't led us wrong? You sure you ain't led us to a house or a line camp?"

"I'm sure. I tell you, Macy, I know where I'm at. There's not a soul lives within miles of here."

The dog barked again a time or two, but Modock couldn't spot the animal in the moonlight. He noticed that the cattle trails began converging, so he satisfied himself Cass was leading them to the tank. Presently he rode up on the dam. A few cattle which were bedded down around the water rose nervously to their feet and began to edge away. Modock whistled. No wonder Blair Bishop was so proud of this tank. Even low, it still held a considerable body of water, enough to keep his cows awhile longer if nothing unexpected happened to it.

Modock was here to see that something did happen to it. He reached into his saddlebags and pulled out three sticks of dynamite. Handing the leather reins to

Owen Darby, he knelt to set the fuses, each a slightly different length. Digging a hole in the dry earth just at the edge of the mud, he laid down the stick with the shortest fuse and packed the earth around it. He walked around the tank, pausing to set a second. At the far side he placed the third, then lighted the long fuse. He came back to the second and touched it off, finished by lighting the first, then took his horse from Darby and swung into the saddle.

"We better move off a ways. These horses will throw a fit."

The first explosion made the earth tremble. Modock's horse tried to pitch. Clarence Cass' simply wanted to run. It was all Cass could do to stop him short of a full stampede. The last two explosions came close together. Modock could hear the mud splatter onto the tank dam. He heard the clatter of cattle stampeding away into the protecting brush.

It took him a minute to get his horse under control, then he forced the reluctant animal back to the tank. Where the charges had been set, Modock saw three sizable holes gradually filling with water. He was counting on the tremors having sent cracks through the tightly packed bottom. They couldn't be seen beneath the water, but Modock was confident they were there. Cass and Owen Darby rode up beside him. Cass said, "The water's still in it."

"It'll take time. Several days, more than likely. But it'll go."

"Bishop'll see them holes. He'll see the mud scattered all over."

"The mud'll dry in the hot sun tomorrow, and the cattle will tromp it back to dust. As for the holes, he can't prove they wasn't pawed by bulls lookin' for a fight."

"In his own mind, he'll know."

"Sure, he'll know." Modock grinned. "I *want* him to know that it's me and not just hard luck. But there won't be a blessed thing he can do about it, not a thing he can prove."

They started back toward the fence, Modock whistling tunelessly, letting his mind run free with all manner of good and violent dreams, the taste of triumph sweet as wild-bee honey.

The dog came charging at them unexpectedly out of the mesquite, barking its challenge. Modock's horse, still unstrung by the explosions, went straight up. Modock took a hard, dirt-eating fall but somehow held on to his reins. He jumped to his feet, holding desperately to the struggling horse. The breath half knocked out of him, Modock managed to slap the barking dog and send it retreating. He cursed, reaching for his pistol but realizing that if he fired a shot, the horse would probably get away from him. He managed finally to get a foot into the stirrup and swing back into the saddle. He spurred the horse viciously, at the same time hauling hard on the reins to keep the animal from getting its head down to buck again.

A voice came from the mesquite. "Macy Modock! I ought to've known it'd be you."

Modock's pistol was in his hand, and he bent low over the horse's neck, hoping not to present an easy target. "Who's that?" he demanded, half panicky at the thought of being caught.

Tank-builder Joe Little rode out of the brush, shotgun pointed toward the three horsemen. He commanded the dog to heel, then approached Modock. The muzzle of that shotgun looked big as a coffeepot. Modock stared in disbelief. "What're you doin' here, Joe?"

"I got a camp over yonder, buildin' another tank for Blair Bishop, below the Black Bull." He glanced contemptuously at Clarence Cass, whose chin had dropped to his shirt collar in the agony of discovery. "First blast woke me up. Thought it was thunder, till I looked up and seen the moon and the stars. The other two blasts come, and all of a sudden I knowed. Raise your hands, Macy. You others too. You'll answer to Blair Bishop."

Modock was recovering from surprise, and he began calculating odds. He didn't like that shotgun. Even if he fired his pistol and hit Joe, he knew the shotgun blast would probably tear him in two. "It's a long ways from here to the Double B headquarters. You better ride off and forget you seen us, Joe."

"I wish I could forget I *ever* seen you, Macy, much less shared a cell with you. It takes a lowdown form of a man to dynamite another man's waterhole and starve his cattle to death. I figure you're goin' back where you come from, Macy, and takin' company with you."

"I made you an offer a while back, Joe. It still stands. Go in with us and get that land you wanted. You might even get some of the Bishop country you been workin' so hard on. Use your head, Joe, and you can wind up bigger than you ever thought of."

"Blair Bishop's a friend of mine. You, Macy, are no friend to anybody." He motioned with the shotgun. "Easy now, and slip them cartridge belts off. Drop them careful."

Modock caught a signal in Owen Darby's face. He couldn't tell exactly what Darby had in mind, but he knew Darby was about to try something. Modock lagged, fumbling with the belt buckle. Darby undid his and slipped the belt and holster loose from his hip as if to drop it. Instead, he flipped it into the face of Joe Little's horse. The horse shied away, forcing Joe involuntarily to grab at the saddle horn and let the shotgun dip.

Modock's right hand streaked back from the buckle and came up with the pistol. He held it almost point-blank at Joe Little's chest. Horror came into Joe's face as he tried desperately to bring the shotgun back into line.

Modock fired. Joe rocked back. His horse jumped in terror. Joe Little slid out of the saddle and hit the ground with one leg crumpled.

Clarence Cass sat stupefied, watching Joe Little gasp away his life. Modock swung to the ground and kicked the shotgun away in case there was still any inclination on Joe's part to use it. But Joe was beyond thinking.

Joe's black dog growled deep in its throat and lunged in fury at Macy Modock. Instinctively Modock threw up his arm. The dog's teeth sank into it. Modock swung the pistol up under the dog's belly and fired. The dog fell away, kicking. Cursing violently, a cold rage flowing over him, Modock fired twice more into the shaggy body.

"Nothin' I hate worse than a damned dog . . ."

He rubbed his arm where the sharp teeth had dug in, bringing blood.

Cass tried to speak, but only a few terrified gasps came. Modock looked up to see Owen Darby catching Joe's runaway horse and bringing it back. Darby looked down at Joe's body. "This sure queers things, Macy. What you goin' to do now?"

Modock shook his head. "I'm tryin' to think. Just shut up and let me study it out." He cursed silently. Damn Joe Little and his stupid meddling. Modock wished Joe hadn't been here; not that he had any regret for the killing itself, but only that it made for an unexpected complication. He had felt no regard for Joe Little when they were in prison together, no more than he felt for anyone else beyond whatever use he might be. It was these unforeseen surprises that always seemed to get a man caught. It was hard to prepare for them.

Modock straightened, deciding he saw a way out. "Owen, you was sayin' the other day you wished you could break into that wooden box of a bank in Two Forks."

Darby nodded. "But you said we had bigger fish to fry, and I might ruin the whole setup."

"All of a sudden I'm changin' my mind. I think it'd be a great idea now for you to bust that bank. Our friend Joe Little was in the pen for doin' that very thing. If he was to disappear right after the bank was robbed, what do you reckon folks would think?"

Darby began to smile. "That's why I like to ride with you, Macy. You can take a disaster and make a winnin' hand out of it."

"We'll take him and his horse and make sure they're never found. Clarence, you get down here and help me with him."

Clarence Cass was almost crying, his throat quivering as he kept trying for voice. He made no move to leave his saddle. Modock railed at him without effect. Darby swung down and helped Modock lift Joe Little's body across the saddle, the frightened horse pulling its head around, its eyes spooked.

Darby asked, "What about our tracks?"

"No way we can rub them all out. We'll just have to hope that nobody will come along till the cattle and the wind have covered them up. Unless somebody's lookin' for tracks, they ain't apt to notice them anyway."

"We can't leave that dog layin' there."

"We'll drag him off into the brush. There won't nobody find him."

Voice came at last to Clarence Cass. "You killed him! You killed him! They'll hang us now for sure!"

Modock glanced at Darby, knowing Darby had been wishing Modock would let him shut the little man up for once and for all. Sooner or later they would have to do something permanent about Cass, but not until all advantage had been taken of him. "Clarence, you quit your cryin'. Get a head back on your shoulders. Anything we done, *you* done."

"I didn't come for no killin'."

"Neither did we, but you got it, and you're in it up to your Adam's apple. Anything that happens to us happens to you too."

"Macy, I didn't know you was goin' to drag me into a thing like this. Just blowin' up a tank was all. That's what you said, just blowin' up a tank. Now I want you off of my ranch, out of this country."

Angrily Modock reached down to Joe Little's warm body and came up with blood thick on his fingers. He smeared it onto Clarence Cass' hand. Cass drew back trembling, trying desperately to wipe the blood onto his trousers. Modock said, "It won't wash off, Clarence. So from now on, your life depends on us. You'll keep your mouth shut and do everything I tell you. Everything! Else you might just wind up where Joe Little is. Come on, let's get out of here!"

VIII

The sun was starting down in the afternoon sky when Sheriff Erly Greenwood and a deputy rode into the yard of the Double B headquarters. Blair Bishop lay on a blanket on the breezy gallery of the ranchhouse, taking gratefully what little comfort he found on a hot summer day. Time had been when his conscience would have hurt him a little, napping like this when there was work to be done. But as the years went by it seemed easier to deal with his conscience on such matters. No matter how much work a man did, it was never enough anyway.

The sound of hoofs brought Blair's gray head up from the pillow. He raised up slowly, stretching, then got to his feet and invited Erly with a broad wave of his hand. "Come on up and shade awhile, Erly. It's hotter than the hinges of hell out in that sun."

Greenwood could well remember when

Blair Bishop wouldn't have taken time for a noonday siesta, but that had been before the ranchman had come to terms with ambition and had learned to accept the natural rhythms of life. He climbed the steps and shook hands with the ranchman. The deputy followed his example. Blair, in his sock feet, led them into the house for a drink of cool water. Then they came back out onto the gallery, for the house caught and held much of the afternoon heat entrapped despite its tall, narrow windows.

"Blair," the sheriff said, "I come to talk to Joe Little."

Blair told him Joe was building a surface tank out close to the Black Bull. Greenwood asked him, "Seen him today?"

"He seldom comes to headquarters, just when he needs somethin'. My boy Billy drops by and keeps him pretty well stocked on groceries and things . . . includin' the best stuff out of my own pantry. What do you want with Joe?"

"Somebody busted into the bank last night. Got off with somethin' like four to five thousand dollars."

"Joe wouldn't . . ." Blair's eyes narrowed. "He paid off what he owed the state. He wouldn't do nothing like that again, Erly. He's got a good job, got friends . . ."

"How long would it take him to make four or five thousand dollars, Blair, workin' a team of mules in this heat, sweatin' himself to death on another man's land? You can see how some of the old quick-money notions might get to preyin' on Joe's mind."

"Did anybody see him?"

"Not exactly. There was a cowboy layin' drunk in an alley. He saw the robber. Said it could have been Joe."

"Could have been? With a drunk cowboy, it *could* have been Ulysses S. Grant or Robert E. Lee."

"Just the same, I sure want to talk to Joe. He's the first one lots of folks in town thought of. If I don't talk to him, some of them are liable to come lookin'."

Blair nodded. "I'll get Billy to hitch a team to the buckboard, and we'll ride with you over there."

They found Joe's camp beside the half-finished tank, the mules hobbled to graze on the scanty grass. Blair Bishop knew the moment he saw the mules that something was wrong. He exchanged glances with Billy and found the same conviction in the boy's eyes. Joe was always working at this time of day. Those mules didn't get the hobbles until sundown. Blair didn't have to say anything. Erly Greenwood read the signs the same way. The sheriff asked, "Does he keep a horse?"

Blair didn't answer, but Billy did. "He's always got a horse. I don't see it anyplace around."

Erly Greenwood's face went grave as he looked over the deserted camp. "You know, don't you, Blair? We'll have to send out word on Joe Little."

Billy protested. "Dad, Joe wouldn't rob nobody. He told me a dozen times he'd rather starve than to do anything like that again."

Blair sensed the desperation in Billy's voice, a silent cry for faith, for Billy had thought the sun rose and set in Joe Little. "Boy," he said unconvincingly, "maybe it's not the way it looks. Maybe old Joe just up and went somewhere."

Erly Greenwood said, "Blair, there's no use kiddin' him. Billy's old enough to take things the way they come." He turned his attention to Billy. "Think hard now, son. Do you remember anything he might've said about places he'd like to go to, things he'd like to do?"

Billy shook his head defensively. "No, sir. He said he was goin' to buy a place of his own. That's all he ever said he wanted, was a place of his own."

The sheriff commented, "Four to five thousand dollars would buy a man a right smart of a little place. He'd have to go a far piece, though. He must've said somethin', Billy."

"Nothin'. I tell you, he didn't say nothin'."

Erly Greenwood studied him apologetically but unconvinced. "All right, son, but if you think of anything later on, let us know. We want to help Joe; we got no wish to hurt him." He shook Blair's hand, gripping it lightly because of the rheumatism, but bringing pain just the same. "Sorry, Blair, I can't say I was in favor of you ever bringin' Joe Little here in the first place, but I'll say this: I liked him."

"You got your job to do, Erly. Want us to help you look for tracks?"

"Any helpful tracks will be the ones goin' *away* from the bank, not the ones he made goin' to it. We'd be wastin' our time out here."

Sitting slumped on the buckboard seat, Blair sorrowfully watched them ride off in the direction of town. The leather lines slacked from Billy's listless hands. Blair looked at his son. "Boy, sometimes life's hard that way. People we like, people we trust, they do things we can't understand, things that hurt us. It don't help to blame them. It ain't right to blame a man unless you try on his boots and walk awhile in his tracks. Whatever was drivin' Joe, it was somethin' more powerful than we know. Ain't right for us to feel hard about him."

"I'm not feelin' hard about him, Dad. I know he didn't do it."

Blair shrugged, not knowing what else to say. "Sometimes we just got to accept the things that are and not ask questions. This is one of those times." He rubbed his aching hand, wanting to busy his mind on other matters and hoping to get Billy occupied too. "Long's we're this close, let's go over and take a look at the Black Bull Tank. It does me good to see a place that's still got water."

The tank's banks were too steep for the buckboard, so Blair climbed heavily out and walked. Billy followed him. At the top of the dam, Blair stopped in surprise. He glanced at Billy, shock in his square face. "Boy, that tank ain't got half the water in it that it had the other day."

Billy's jaw dropped. "I was over here just day before yesterday. It still had lots of water in it. Somethin's happened. It's gone plumb to hell."

That wasn't language Blair had taught

Billy to use, though he used it liberally enough himself. He never even noticed this time. In dismay he trudged down toward the water line. He bogged in heavy black mud almost to his boottops. "Right here's where the water line was a day or two ago. Cattle didn't drink this much, and it don't evaporate this fast."

He knelt painfully, touching the wet ground with his hand as if somehow that would give him a hint to what had gone wrong. He got up slowly, feeling as if a mule had kicked him in the stomach. Billy looked at him in alarm. For a moment Blair thought Billy's expression was a reflection of his concern over the water, but he realized that wasn't it, at least not the main part of it.

Billy said, "Dad, you better go sit in the buckboard awhile. You've turned as white as skim milk."

"I'm all right, boy, I'm all right." Blair looked at the water again, still mystified. He started around the edge of it, looking for a line that might indicate a crack in the dam. He didn't see anything.

He didn't see the hole, either, until he fell into it and went to his knees. Billy ran to help him, but Blair pushed to his feet alone, wiping the mud from his hands onto his already muddy trousers. "Damned bulls," he muttered, "pawin' holes where a man can fall in them. If they ever come up with a substitute, I'll never have a bull on the place again."

Billy observed, "They been doin' a lot of fightin', seems like. There's another bull hole over yonder."

"Bunch of bulls around here are sure in need of a shippin'," Blair growled. Pawing holes was bull nature, but at a time like this Blair had no patience with it. He glanced across the tank and became aware of a third hole which looked about like the other two. Of a sudden, suspicion hit him. The impact was almost as hard as the initial one of seeing the tank nearly dry.

"Billy, somethin' strike you funny about them bull holes?"

Billy shook his head. "Nothin' strikes me very funny right now."

"Aside from the fact that there's three of them showed up all at the same time, and the fact that they're kind of deep, don't it seem peculiar to you that they're in the edge of the mud instead of out where the sand is a little dryer? An old bull ain't goin' to stand and paw mud when there's dry ground all around him."

Billy blinked in confusion. "What you tryin' to say, Dad?"

"I'm not sure. It's just a feelin' that's come over me, or maybe somethin' I smell. There's more here than meets the eye."

"You think Joe Little went and did somethin'? He wouldn't, Dad. He wouldn't hurt us thisaway."

"Not Joe Little. I was thinkin' of Macy Modock."

"Joe would've known about it. He'd of told us . . ." Billy's eyes widened as the implication hit him. "Unless Modock done somethin' to him." He grabbed his father's arm. "Dad, we got to catch up to Erly Greenwood and tell him."

"Tell him what? We'd have to prove it first."

"But maybe Joe's in trouble and needs our help. No tellin' what that Modock might be doin' to him."

Blair knew now. Though he had nothing stronger than instinct to go by, he knew. "Whatever it is, boy, he's already done it. Macy Modock is a hard man. Whatever he felt like he had to do to Joe, it's over and done with."

"You think he killed him?"

"You'd best make up your mind to it, Billy. I'll bet everything I own. If Modock was out here and Joe caught him, then Joe is dead."

Billy's hands trembled as the enormity of the idea took hold. Tears welled into his eyes. "Then let's go after Modock. Let's kill him!"

Blair Bishop firmly took his son's arm. "No, son, that's not for us to do. Time was when it would've been the thing, but that time is gone. We'll go tell Erly Greenwood what we think. The fixin' of it is up to him."

"Joe Little was our friend."

Blair Bishop's eyes were bleak, and he knew a moment of temptation. "If I was your age and time was rolled back a few years, I'd do just what you're sayin'. But I ain't, and it ain't, and we can't. Let's get to the buckboard. If we push, maybe we can catch Erly."

They did, and Greenwood came back for a look around. What he saw did not incline him to agree. "I don't see a thing that supports you, Blair. If there was any tracks, they're gone. If them holes was blowed or dug, there's nothin' to show for it. For all I can tell, they're just what they look like . . . a sign the bulls was fightin'. The trouble with you and Billy is that you don't want to accept the truth when it stares you in the eye. Joe Little got tired of workin' and robbed that bank. You've got Macy Modock so heavy on your mind that you're ready to blame him for everything but the drought. If he's tryin' to make you sweat, he's doin' a good job of it. I bet you ain't slept a full night in peace since he came back. Now he's givin' you nightmares in the daytime."

That was strong talk coming from Erly Greenwood, who had always handled Blair Bishop with a respectful deference. But Greenwood had a looted bank in town to worry about, and the weather was hot, and he'd made a lot of extra miles that weren't taking him any closer to the man who had done the job.

Angered, Blair said, "I got a strong feelin' about this thing, Erly. You won't find Joe Little, not on this earth. If you want to find that bank money, you go to Macy Modock."

Greenwood kept his impatience in check; Blair had to give him credit for that. "Blair, I'll see you again soon's I get some time. Awful sorry about that tank."

IX

The Black Bull Tank had become only a mudhole. Blair had known that as soon as he had seen the cattle standing around the tankdam. There had been far too many for this early in the day. Usually they began gathering in the afternoon and watered, then lay around until the cool of the evening brought them back to their feet and set them to looking for grass. Blair could tell these cattle had been here since yesterday, and they were thirsty. He rode up on the dam, his two sons flanking him. What he saw confirmed his fears.

"Well, it's gone, boys. The trap's drawin' shut."

Allan nodded gravely. Billy stared, the consequences not quite so apparent to him as to his father and his older brother. "We'll just have to take them somewhere else," he said.

Blair Bishop nodded sourly, still convinced

Modock had brought this trouble on him. "It means we'll have to double up cattle on another place that's already in trouble itself." He pondered a moment. "We'll haze them over onto the Harley Mills pasture. At least there we got a couple of windmill's still pumpin' all right."

Allan said, "Grass is awful short over there, Dad."

"It's short everywhere. But there's water, at least." He rode down the dam, waving his hand and hollering at the cattle. His sons fanned out on either side of him and did likewise. One cow remained. She was out twenty feet in the mud, hopelessly mired to her belly. Trembling, she shook her head angrily at the horsemen. She had obviously been here for some time, struggling vainly, fighting this mud. She was in a hostile mood toward all the world.

"Allan," Blair called, "I graduated from this kind of chore a long time ago. I'll let you do the honors. Billy, you keep gatherin' the rest of them cattle."

Allan stepped to the ground and tightened his cinch for a good pull. He rode to the edge of the mud, swung his loop and sailed it around the cow's horns. Taking up the slack, he dallied the end of the rope around his saddle horn and spurred away. The horse

101

scrambled for footing, pulling hard. The cow's neck stretched and she bawled in rage, but the mud held her.

Blair said, "I was afraid it wouldn't be that easy. You'll have to get in there with her. Hand me your rope."

Allan took it philosophically, for this was part of a cowboy's work. Using a few choice words to describe the ancestry of a brute stupid enough to get herself into such a predicament, he took off his boots and waded into the mud.

Blair's horse was bigger and stronger than Allan's. Blair always rode a big horse, for he was an older and heavier man. He dallied Allan's rope around his saddle horn. The cow slung her head, trying vainly to reach Allan with her horns. He got behind her and grasped her tail. Blair spurred. As the horse strained against the rope, Allan lifted the cow's hindquarters. The first try didn't move her much, but on the second she somehow got her feet under her and began adding to the struggle what little strength she had left. She moved forward gradually at first. Then she broke loose from the mud's tight grip and came scrambling up out of it. On dry ground, she went to her knees. Her tongue was hanging out, and she was bawling in rage. Allan eased up to get the rope off, but she was ready to fight anything which moved. She slung her head and missed him only an inch with her sharp horns. Allan dodged back, cursing her. She got to her feet and charged him. There was nothing for Allan to do but run toward his horse, barefoot, muddy to his thighs. The horse didn't like the looks of either him or the cow, and he shied away.

Blair put his own horse between Allan and the cow and took another dally farther down on the rope. He rode away fast, jerking the cow off of her feet. While she was down, Allan slipped the rope off. He lost no time picking up his boots and getting back into his saddle. He would stay barefoot till the mud dried enough that he could rub it off.

Blair and Allan watched the cow slowly struggle to her feet. She stood shaking, tongue out and drooling saliva as she faced them in frustration and anger, tossing her head in belligerence.

"Never fails to happen," Allan said. "Do one a favor, and she turns on you."

"Female. A lot of females will do you that way. Cow, human, or whatever."

The cow decided she had made her point, and she moved weakly up over the dam to seek out her sisters. Allan looked at his father. "You tryin' to say somethin', Dad?"

Blair shrugged. "Yep, and you know what it is."

"I told you before, Dad, there's no use us talkin' about Jessie. Nothin' you say is goin' to change the way I feel about her. And I'm goin' to keep right on seein' her. I wish you wouldn't crowd me."

"If it was just seein' her, boy, that wouldn't be so bad. But it's more than that. One of these times you'll feel called upon to marry her. Sure, she looks pretty good to you now, mostly because you ain't seen a lot of other girls and got nothin' to compare by. I swear, I'd almost rather see you spendin' your time down on Silky Row in town. At least nobody there would try to tie on to you. Everybody would know just where she stood."

Allan stopped his horse. He looked his father in the eye, a quality Blair had taught him from the time he was big enough to walk. "Dad, I never lied to you, and I won't lie to you now. When the time is right, I'm goin' to marry Jessie Cass. Now, you can accept her, or you can tell us both to leave. I hope you'll accept her, because she's a good girl. But even if you don't, that won't change anything. I'll marry her. You won't stand in my way, and neither will anybody else."

Blair Bishop felt anger. He had raised his boys not to talk back to him. But he had also taught them to be straightforward and not back off from a problem. Blair struggled to put down his anger. Allan didn't seem to be in any hurry about this. Maybe something would come along to help Blair open his eyes for him before it was too late.

Blair retreated, but he didn't surrender. "Billy's probably havin' trouble tryin' to push them cattle all by himself. We better go give him a hand."

Along the way they picked up foreman Finn Goforth and cowboy Hez Northcutt, who had been riding missions of their own. The cattle drove sluggishly at first, their thirst making them contrary, and their instincts tugging them back toward the tank where they were used to watering. Every so often an animal would turn back, and only a rope would stop her. Billy was the one who most often used the rope. He was at an age when a rope had a rough appeal to him and nothing was so much fun as to stand a runaway steer on its rump. Irritably, for he was thirsty too, Blair grouched at him about rough-handling the stock. Billy would explain that he couldn't afford to let them get away.

They missed dinner, for moving these

cattle to water was more important than getting back to the headquarters for a noon meal. A cowboy was conditioned to accept such things. The good of the stock was always paramount over the needs of the man.

Late in the afternoon the tall windmill showed on the short-grass prairie. It seemed to shimmer and dance in the heatwaves playing along the horizon. Riding point, Blair Bishop thought he saw a cloud of dust ahead of him, and the movement of cattle. He blinked and lost sight of it in the heat. Eyesight going bad, he decided. Looked like when the rheumatism got hold of him, it was bound to take everything else. By now he was tired and hot and thirsty and irritable. So was everybody else on the drive. He hadn't heard a man speak a word in an hour, except to use the Lord's name in vain against some recalcitrant critter.

But directly Finn Goforth trotted his horse up from the flank and pulled in beside Blair. "Do you see somethin' odd up ahead of us?"

Blair grunted. "Thought I did, but I lost it. Mirage, I figured, or just my own eyes. Times anymore I'm not worth killin'."

Finn pointed. "It ain't no mirage."

Blair sat up straight in the saddle. He

stared a moment, glanced at Finn in disbelief and looked back again. "Finn, somebody's movin' cattle."

"There's nothin' up yonder but Double B range. There's not anybody supposed to be movin' cattle here but us."

Anger surged red into Blair's square face. "Rustlers! In broad open daylight!"

Finn Goforth shook his head. "That's the first thought that came to me. You know we been losin' some cattle lately, a few here, a few there. Started about the time Macy Modock come back. But they'd have to have a lot of gall to come so far onto Double B country in the daytime when there'd be so much chance of a Bishop man runnin' onto them. I can't hardly believe they'd be stealin' cattle now. Tonight, maybe, after the moon comes up, but not now."

By instinct Blair Bishop reached for his hip. He didn't have a pistol, hadn't worn one in years. He looked back at his two sons and Hez Northcutt. "Nary a gun in the whole bunch of us, Finn, except that carbine you carry under your leg. Let me have it, and I'll ride up and see what the hell is goin' on."

Goforth shook his head. "With that hand of yours, you couldn't lever it. One shot is all you'd ever get. I'll go with you, Mister

107

Bishop, and I'll keep hold of the rifle."

Blair flexed his right hand. It was painfully stiff. Finn was right. Blair looked over his shoulder and signaled for Allan to come up on the run. He could tell that Allan had seen the other string of cattle too. "You go tell Billy and Hez to keep pushin' this bunch. The three of us are ridin' on to see what this is all about."

He swung into an easy lope that would give Allan a chance to catch up with him. The thought fleetingly crossed his mind that if it *was* cow thieves, and they were armed, one saddlegun wouldn't be much persuasion against them. But the thought was not enough to slow him. It had been said of Blair Bishop in his younger days that he would charge hell with a bucket of gypwater. Armed or not, he had seen few men who would stand against him long.

Between the three men and the windmill lay a barbed wire fence. Originally the four sections of land where the windmill stood had been homesteaded at Blair's suggestion by Harley Mills when Harley was a Double B cowboy. He had gone through the state requirements, then had sold the place to Blair and gone off to get gloriously drunk. He had never been completely sober since, and Blair had been obliged to fire him.

Next to the Mills land was a similar place Blair had bought from a homesteading cowboy named Abernathy. Unlike Mills, Abernathy had taken his money and bought a string of steers. He threw them in with a trail herd bound for the railroad and was drowned trying to swim a creek. In his honor the land was still known as the Abernathy place, though it had been in the Bishop name for years.

A double-width wire gate was marked by three tall posts. Blair moved toward them, but he saw other riders were going to get there first from the far side of the fence. Behind the riders came a large herd of slow-moving cattle, obscured by heavy gray dust. Blair recognized a tall, gaunt man whose black hat was pulled down almost over his eyes. "That's Macy Modock. Let me have that rifle, Finn."

Goforth demurred again. "I don't want to see you killed, Mister Bishop, so I better keep it. Any time you want him shot, just give me the word."

Someone dismounted and threw the two gates wide open, then climbed back onto his horse. Macy Modock pulled up into one of the gates and stopped, waiting. Beside him was the red-bearded one Blair remembered as Owen Darby. Darby had a saddlegun lying across the pommel of his saddle. Two other riders flanked them, facing toward the Bishops and Finn Goforth. None looked much like preachers.

Macy Modock held up his hand as Blair Bishop neared. It wasn't a gesture of peace; it was a sign to stop.

"Macy," Blair spoke angrily, "this here is my land, and I'll wager them yonder is my cattle. Now what the hell are you up to?"

Modock gave him that dry, flat, dangerous smile of his. "You're right, Blair Bishop, up to a point. Them is your cattle, and that where you're at is your land. But this where I'm sittin', it's not your land anymore; it's mine. I'm movin' your cattle off of it."

The surprise struck Blair Bishop like a fist. He hesitated, wondering if the thirst and the heat hadn't affected his hearing. "Your land? It's mine, and it has been for years."

Macy Modock patiently shook his head. That smile clung, ugly and threatening. "You thought it was. You thought you had defrauded the state. But after all this time you been caught up with, Bishop. You're losin' it, and I've filed claim on it."

Finn Goforth held the carbine. "Just say the word, Mister Bishop . . ."

If Blair had held the rifle at that moment,

he probably would have shot Macy Modock out of the saddle, or tried to. But he didn't and perhaps that helped him take a better look at the three men who sided Modock. Finn's first shot would have to be a good one; he would never live to fire a second. "Stay easy, Finn," Blair rasped. He had no wish to lose a good foreman and longtime friend. To Modock he said, "If you think I'm goin' to stand still for you takin' four good sections of my land . . ."

Macy shook his head. "Not four . . . *eight.* Them other four sections yonder was filed on by a feller name of Abernathy. You're losin' those too. Owen here has filed on that land."

Blair flamed, "You're not bluffin' us, Macy. We got thirsty cattle comin', and you're standin' in the gate. Pull aside."

Macy's hand moved back near the pistol at his hip. "The only cattle passin' through that gate is the ones behind us, and they're goin' out, not in."

"Those eight sections have got about all the dependable water left on this ranch, Macy. They're the only place, almost, where a man can find well water just about any- where he digs. I'm not givin' them up to nobody."

"You don't have to give them up; they're

bein' *took.* You see, Bishop, you thought I was the only enemy you had. You thought when you sent me up that you didn't have any enemy left who could hurt you. But you didn't think about Judge Quincy. A little old dried-up wart like that couldn't do you no damage, you thought. But you wasn't payin' attention."

Blair Bishop listened, stewing.

Modock went on: "This land was homesteaded by Abernathy and Mills. They swore they met all the state's requirements, and they got the deeds. But did you ever look at the fine print on them papers, Bishop? No, of course you didn't. You thought anything a Bishop could get his hands on was safe forever. But there's fine print that says if there's fraud in connection with them homesteads, they can be taken back and put up for somebody else to claim."

"There wasn't no fraud."

"It was common knowledge around here that you was in collusion with them cowboys when they filed on that land. Before they ever done it, they agreed to sell the land to you. You held them to it."

"There never was any such agreement. I told them when the time came I'd like to buy and would pay them a good price. I never told them they had to. There was a

112

couple who didn't. They're still my friends."

Finn Goforth was one of them, but Blair saw no need mentioning the fact to the likes of Macy Modock. Finn had decided he wanted to keep his land as something to build on for his own future. He was still working for Blair, letting Blair use his land under lease and letting the lease payments stack up as savings in the Two Forks bank to buy a cow herd someday.

Modock said, "We got a signed affidavit from Harley Mills. He says him and Abernathy never actually lived on their land the way they was supposed to. They lived in the Double B bunkhouse the whole blessed time."

"They both set up shacks on their land. They lived in them the way the law specified."

"I ain't seen no shacks."

"We taken them down and reused the lumber."

Modock grunted sarcastically. "Sure. That'd sound good in court. Can you produce either man to swear he lived in the shack?"

"You know Abernathy's dead. As for Harley Mills, he'd sell his soul for a barrel of whiskey. How much did you give him?"

"Harley says you got him to swear false

113

testimony, then forced him to sell to you or you'd expose him and get him sent to jail."

"Harley lied. He lived up to the law, same as the others. He taken his money and drank it up. That's why he's swampin' a stable."

"He claims you got what you wanted from him and then fired him."

"I had to let him go because he was drinkin' too much. You better not depend on Harley for a witness. He'll be drunk when you need him."

"I got his affidavit. What have *you* got, Bishop? I tell you what you *ain't* got; you ain't got this land no more. *We* have. And we're movin' you off it today."

Finn Goforth said deliberately, "No you ain't," and he raised the saddlegun. That was a mistake. Owen Darby's carbine fired. The horses jumped in fright. Blair saw Finn rock back in the saddle, discharging his carbine harmlessly in the air. He doubled over and slid to the ground.

"Finn!" Blair shouted. He tried to dismount, but his big gray was crow-hopping excitedly. Blair's stiff legs went out from under him as he hit the ground, and he went down on hands and knees almost under the panicked gray horse. A hoof barely missed him before Blair could crawl away and struggle painfully to his feet.

Allan was already on his knees beside the foreman and was turning Finn over. Finn's face was going gray. Blood flowed from a wound deep in his shoulder.

Blair picked up Finn's fallen carbine. He tried feverishly to lever a fresh cartridge into the breech, but his crippled hand betrayed him. He couldn't get a grip. He cursed wildly, furious at the hand, furious at Macy Modock. But the hand wouldn't function. Forcing it brought only pain.

Glancing up, he saw three men's guns leveled at him and knew that if he had been able to lever a cartridge, they would not have let him live to fire it.

Macy Modock raised his hand and motioned for his men to lower their weapons. "Not yet, boys, not yet. Comes time to do the honors on Blair Bishop, I want to do it myself."

Blair stood openmouthed and raging, the sweat rolling down his dusty face, pain lancing through his hand from trying to force it to do something of which it no longer was capable. "Modock, I swear to God . . ."

"Just go on and swear, Bishop. Ain't another damn thing you can do."

Allan's anxious voice reached Blair. "Dad, Finn's hard hit. He won't live long if we don't get this blood stopped."

A cold chill ran through Blair Bishop as he realized how close he had come to being killed, standing there with that useless rifle in his hands. He dropped it and turned back to Finn Goforth. Allan ripped Finn's shirt open to expose the wound.

Billy Bishop and Hez Northcutt had abandoned their cattle at the sound of the shot and came loping up excitedly. Hez jumped off to see about Finn. Billy glanced at Finn, saw the blood, then spotted the saddlegun lying on the ground. He reached for it, but Blair managed to grab him.

"Boy, don't touch that rifle! Can't you see they're fixin' to kill you?"

Billy cried in fury: "He's the one that killed Joe Little. Now he's shot Finn."

Macy Modock said coldly, "Go on, Blair Bishop, let him pick it up."

Blair sensed they wouldn't withhold fire against Billy. They would cut him to pieces. Blair pushed Billy back, putting himself between the gunmen and his son. "No, Modock, you're not goin' to get at me by killin' these boys of mine."

Allan methodically wadded a handkerchief against Finn's wound, trying to stop the blood. When that handkerchief was soaked, Blair handed him one from his own pocket.

If the wound didn't kill Finn, those dirty handkerchiefs probably would, Blair thought darkly.

"Billy, you and Hez ride up to the ranch. Billy, you go to town and fetch a doctor to the house. Get word to the sheriff too. Hez, you load up the buckboard with blankets and bring it here in a run. Allan and I'll take care of him the best we can till you get back."

Billy said, "How about them cows?"

"The hell with the cows. We got to save Finn."

The young cowboys rode off together in a lope that Blair knew was likely to kill both horses if they didn't slow down. They would, when excitement gave way to judgment. Allan and Blair carried the foreman gently to the shade of a thin mesquite tree and laid him on the ground. The blood gradually stopped.

On the other side of the gate, the riders arrived with the cattle they were pushing for Macy Modock. Blair watched in helpless anger as they drove them through the double gate and then chased them into a run that would carry them a considerable distance out across a waterless pasture.

Modock rode over and looked down from the saddle, the hard smile still making a slash across his thin face. "Too bad about your man. Owen Darby's slippin' in his old age. Time was when he'd have got this feller in the heart and you wouldn't have to be fussin' over him thisaway. You'd just dig a hole for him, is all."

"Did you dig a hole for Joe Little?"

Modock never changed expression. "You ain't found it, have you?"

Blair said, "Soon's I get Finn took care of, I'll be back. I'll bring plenty with me."

Modock was unmoved. "It ain't your land no more. It's mine, or fixin' to be. Judge Quincy's been over at the Statehouse the last four days. I got a wire from him that he had everything fixed. That land is mine and Owen Darby's. We're goin' to put the Cass cattle on it."

"They don't just take a man's land away without goin' to court."

"If you want to press it, I reckon you can have your day in court. But you'll lose. Judge tells me that's a cinch. And meantime, as they say, possession is nine points of the law. I sure as hell got possession. And I got some boys yonder tough enough to see that I keep it."

"Without that land, I got a bunch of cows that don't have water to drink. You won't keep me off."

"Seems to me I heard about my partner Clarence Cass tryin' to tell you he had the same problem. And I remember what you told him. So I'm tellin' you the same thing, Blair Bishop, with one extra addition: any of your men tries to come onto my land, I'm givin' my boys orders to shoot him."

Blair Bishop stared at Finn's saddlegun, still lying where it had been dropped. From here, if Allan would lever a cartridge into it for him, Blair was almost sure he could shoot Macy Modock as the man rode away. Blair made a move toward the rifle then stopped, knowing he couldn't do it that way.

He might curse himself the rest of his life for missing the chance, but he couldn't shoot a man in the back. Not even Macy Modock.

X

For the better part of an hour the doctor labored in flickering light while first one man then another held a lamp close. But finally he straightened in resignation, wiping a handkerchief over his bald head and his sweat-glistening face. "I'm sorry, Blair. Did all I could, but Finn Goforth is gone."

Cold lay in the pit of Blair's stomach. Even as he had paced the parlor floor, pausing periodically to stare blackly out into the darkness, he had known it would end this way.

The doctor said, "If I'd been close by when it happened, maybe I could've saved him. Even then it would've been close." He began putting his instruments into his bag.

"Doc," Blair rasped, wanting comfort and not knowing where to find it, "it's midnight. No use you ridin' to town now. We got a bed for you and a couple of stiff drinks to help settle you if you need them." The doctor nodded his acceptance. "God knows I need them."

Blair added, "Could be we'll need you again anyway. When we've done right by Finn, we'll be goin' back over there."

"With the few men you've got?"

"I'll have more. I'm fixin' to send the boys out to round up all the friends we can muster."

The doctor poured a liberal drink out of a bottle Blair fetched from a cabinet. He sat down wearily, taking one stiff drink that twisted his face, then sipping easier on the rest of it while he pondered. "You have two sons, Blair. Tomorrow one of them — maybe both — could be lyin' here where Finn is."

"It's our land. It'll be the boys' land one of these days . . ." Blair rubbed his cramped, aching hand. "Maybe not so long off."

"Your land. And you'd expect your friends to come and die for it with you? That's a lot to ask of friendship, Blair."

"No more than I've done for some of them." He didn't have to tell the doctor how it had been in earlier days, about the Comanche raids and the like. Doc knew. "This fight ain't just for me or my boys; it's for all these people. You remember how bad it used to be when Macy Modock was here before.

If we let him get a foothold, it'll be the same way again."

"You're still not the law, Blair. We've got a duly elected sheriff in this county. It's up to him to handle it."

Blair's left fist doubled. His right one couldn't. "Erly can't do it all by himself." He turned to his sons, to Hez Northcutt and to chunky Chaco Martinez. "Saddle up. You got some ridin' to do."

He stepped out onto the gallery with them. From the darkness came the sound of a running horse. Blair motioned for the others to wait. "Could be the sheriff," he said. Nobody had been able to find him earlier. The lawman was still scouring the country for Joe Little.

The horse loped into the open yard, and Blair saw the flare of long skirts. He frowned as Jessie Cass reined to a stop and jumped down in front of the house. Her eyes went straight to Allan. "Allan," she cried, "are you all right?"

Allan hurried down the steps and grabbed her into his arms. "Jessie, what're you doin' here?"

"I heard them say they'd shot somebody. They didn't say who. I was scared to death it was you. I'd of died if it was you."

Blair Bishop watched hard-eyed as Allan

held the girl tightly. "It was Finn. He's dead, Jessie."

"Dead?" She sobbed quietly. "I've been afraid it would come to somethin' like this. I've been tryin' to tell Dad . . ."

Blair moved stiffly down the steps. His voice was cold.

"You go on home, girl, and you tell your daddy somethin' else. You tell him he picked himself the wrong partners if he has any notion of gettin' his greedy hands on some of the Double B for them scrubby cattle. You tell him a good man died here tonight, and I'm holdin' him responsible right along with the others."

Jessie turned from Allan, but she still held his hand. "He can't do anything," she said brokenly. "All those men . . . bad men . . . they've got him scared to open his mouth. They're breakin' him down, Mister Bishop. They've taken over."

"He asked for it. He let it start. I got no sympathy for Clarence Cass, but one thing I'll sure as hell promise him: I'm goin' to protect what's mine. He ain't goin' to get any of this land, either by stealin' it or by marryin' off his daughter to it. If I got to bury your old daddy along with the rest of them, then that's just what I'll do. You go tell him that, girl."

"Please, Mister Bishop, you've got to understand how it is . . ."

"I *know* how it is. I lost one good man findin' out. I got a strong hunch I lost another and just can't prove it. So you go tell him what I said. Tell him if he's got half the brains God gave a jackrabbit, he'll pack up and leave this country on the fastest horse he's got. And you better go with him."

Allan tightened his hold on the girl's hand. "Jessie's not goin'."

Blair's eyes narrowed. He gave the girl a long, hard look, then turned to Allan. He thrust his jaw forward. "Boy, we got a good man dead in yonder. I don't want to ever see Clarence Cass' miserable whinin' face again, and I won't have this girl around to remind me of him." To the stricken girl he said evenly, "Now get on that horse and go home, girl. Don't you ever come here again!"

Crying, she tried to leave. Allan held her. Stubbornly he faced his father. "I've told you how it is with us. Anywhere Jessie goes, I go with her!"

That shook Blair Bishop. He said, "You know what we got to do tomorrow. If we don't do it, Finn died for nothin'. Would you turn your back on us at a time like this?"

"Not unless I was forced to it. Don't you

force me."

"The choice is yours. I don't want that girl here. Not now and not ever."

Allan eyed his father an awful moment, then the girl. He gripped Jessie's hand so hard she flinched. "Jessie, I got a duty here. I'll see it through. When it's done, I'll come for you and we'll *both* leave this country. You go on home and get your things ready. Chances are I'll be there sometime tomorrow."

Blair Bishop swallowed, but he tried not to let the bitter disappointment show. He turned away from the couple and walked out into the yard, struggling for control over the grief and anger which shook him. He could hear Allan talking softly to the girl. "He's speakin' for himself," Allan was saying, "but not for me. Soon as I go to fetch you, you can say goodbye to that place. You won't ever have to go back there."

Blair didn't look, but he could tell Allan was helping the girl onto her horse. "Allan," she said, "be careful. Those men had as soon kill you as look at you. Maybe a little rather."

"I'll be careful. You do the same."

The horse moved away. Presently Blair heard his oldest son walk up beside him. "She's gone, Dad, and you won't have to look at her again. Soon's we get this quarrel with Modock over with, I'll be leavin'."

"It's your choice to make, son," Blair said stiffly.

"Always remember, I didn't want to make it."

By daylight the first people came. A neighbor brought a pine coffin that he had stayed up through the post-midnight hours to build. His wife had padded the interior of it with dark velvet cloth. The men filed through the Bishop parlor to view Finn Goforth in the simple coffin. Then they gathered on the gallery in angry silence, for Finn had been a man without an enemy, except those he inherited through Blair Bishop.

Blair sat in the parlor quietly receiving the people. Few women came, because what lay ahead this day was for the men to do. Nobody talked about it, but Blair sensed it was strong on everyone's mind. Mentally he tallied the men as they arrived. About ten o'clock he pushed painfully to his feet. He looked a minute into the faces of men he counted as friends — ranchers, cowboys, people from town. They had come to side him in his hour of need, for they realized it was their hour too.

Allan Bishop waited with the rest. Blair

wished that he could undo what had been said in the dark of night, but it lay between them like a strong adobe wall. He nodded at Allan. "Let's go, son."

Billy Bishop came out of his bedroom, shotgun in hand.

Blair caught his arm. "Billy, you're not of age for this. When we've finished buryin' Finn, you're comin' back to the house."

"I'm old enough. There's not nobody can shoot this thing any better."

Blair's voice carried in it a firmness that plainly brooked no argument. "You're stayin' home, son."

The burial was soon over. Without saying anything, Blair Bishop limped out and swung heavily upon his big gray horse. The other men followed suit. The only sound was of stamping hoofs and creaking leather. For a moment Blair caught the reluctant look in Billy's eyes. Blair wanted to know *one* son would be home when he came back . . . if he came back.

He set out with a dozen riders behind him. Before he had gone a mile, he picked up three more. They moved in a stiff trot, saving the horses but steadily putting the miles behind them. Blair led them in an arc that would allow them to pick up most of the cattle. The ones Modock had herded out of the pasture probably would be scattered in the general vicinity of the gate, wanting back in for the water they were accustomed to. The others which Blair and the men had driven yesterday probably would be strung out halfway to the Black Bull Tank by now, instinct taking them back.

The horsemen picked up the scattered cattle as they found them and bunched them gradually, pushing toward the double gates. The animals were dry now, slobbering for want of water. They moved sluggishly, instinct telling them they were being pushed away from water rather than toward it. The dry ground went to powder beneath the scraping of their sharp hoofs, and dust rose in a choking veil of gray.

Finally Blair could see the tall gateposts which marked the location of the fence. And he could see the dark figures he knew were horsemen, waiting to stop them. "This time, Macy Modock," he muttered, "you'll move aside or get trampled."

The day was hot, but the sweat which broke over him was cold. He counted the men at the gate. Six. He had them outnumbered by more than two to one. He said nothing. He simply touched spurs to the big gray and moved into an easy swinging lope, leaving the cattle. Without looking back, he knew the men behind him would follow his lead. The thought gave him satisfaction, knowing he had friends strong enough in their faith to follow him into the muzzles of professional guns. But the responsibility was heavy too. For half a moment he felt the hard tug of strong doubt. But this left him in a rise of bitterness as he recognized the thin form of Macy Modock slacked on his horse just beyond the wire gate.

Blair pulled a shotgun out of his saddle scabbard. He had left his rifle at home because he feared his right hand would allow him poor use of it, at best. But he could handle this shotgun. For one shot, at least. He would make that shot a good one, or he would never get a second.

His horsemen pulled up on either side of him, presenting a broad, massive line bristling with weapons. Blair studied the men across the fence. Each had a rifle or a pistol in his hands. Mostly rifles.

We can't help but win, he thought, *but there's liable to be some good men fall.*

The alternative was to be able to convince Modock of the hopelessness of his situation, and failing this, to get Modock with a first shot that might — given luck — be the only one fired. One more man dead among

Blair's good friends was one more man too many.

Maybe Modock would see reason when he looked into all those guns.

One of the wire gates lay on the ground, thrown back out of the way. A horseman rode through it, his hand raised. Blair felt surprise. This was sheriff Erly Greenwood.

"Erly," Blair said, "my boy told me he couldn't find you last night."

"I got in awful late. What I found didn't cheer me none. Blair, you got to call this off."

"*Me?* You get Macy Modock to call it off. He's the one makin' the grab, startin' the trouble."

Erly Greenwood appeared considerably agitated. Blair surmised he had been arguing with Macy Modock before the ranchers arrived. He probably hadn't gotten anywhere with Modock. *The only thing Modock understands is a .30-.30 slug, or a dose of buckshot,* Blair thought.

The sheriff appeared almost in despair. Blair hadn't slept any last night, and he guessed the sheriff hadn't either. Greenwood said, "Blair, you got to back off. Somebody'll get killed here sure as hell."

Blair shook his head. "I come to put my cows back where they belong. They're goin'

130

through that gate, Erly, before the sun's an hour higher."

"You got good men with you. Friends of yours, friends of mine. You don't want their blood on your conscience."

"They know what's at stake here. They know what it might cost. They figure this is for them as well as for me. Them thirsty cows back yonder are mine. But next week or next month they could be somebody else's. We've decided we're goin' to stop the thing before it ever really starts. We'll stop it here."

"I'm askin' you to back away, Blair."

Blair frowned, beginning to be puzzled. "You askin' me as a friend, Erly, or as the sheriff?"

"As a friend first. If you won't do it as a friend, then I'll ask you as the sheriff."

"Them cows yonder, they can't wait much longer. They're dry. I'm takin' them to water. That's my land."

"Maybe it's not, Blair."

Blair stared, incredulous. "You better explain that."

"Judge Quincy got in from the Statehouse. Brought a court order with him. It's an injunction to keep you off till there can be a hearin' on whether you got legal title or not."

"Legal title? I've had title for years."

"Seems like Quincy dug up somethin' that casts a shadow over your deeds, Blair. The court orders everything held still till there can be a hearin'. Now, I'm askin' you again to turn back."

"Erly, you wouldn't side with Modock."

"You know me better than that. But I got to uphold the law, and a court order's the law. So back off, Blair, please."

"And if I don't?"

"Then I got to try and stop you."

"You wouldn't shoot me, Erly."

"But I might block that gate till you shoot *me*."

Dry-mouthed, Blair looked awhile at Erly Greenwood, then at the barbed wire fence and at the windmill far beyond it. He looked at the riders who faced him across that fence, and most of all he stared at Macy Modock, the hatred aboil in him.

"This is twice now you've let me down, Erly."

"Not through any choice of mine, Blair. I'd resign this badge before I'd hurt you. Right now I'm just tryin' to keep you from hurtin' yourself."

"What about my cows?"

"You push them up to the gate and I'll make Modock drive them to the mill for water, then bring them back to you. But you keep your men on this side."

"One waterin' saves them for one day. What about tomorrow?"

"I don't know, Blair. Honest to God, I don't know what you're goin' to do about this problem."

"Modock may not want to water them even this once."

"Right now he needs the law. He's usin' me and knows it. I'll tell him he'll do it or I'll shoot him."

Blair pondered, all his instincts telling him to fight, to make this a showdown and get it over with while the odds heavily favored him. Another time, they might be heavily against him. He studied the guns across the fence and felt his hands cold-sweaty against his own shotgun.

We could do it, he thought, wanting to go ahead. *We could do it so easy . . .*

He watched Macy Modock running his ready hand up and down the rifle he held lying across the pommel of his saddle, its muzzle vaguely pointed in Blair's direction. Blair gauged the distance and knew he would have to move closer for this shotgun to take good effect.

To move closer, he would have to ride over Erly Greenwood.

Blair looked to one side of him, then to the other, at the men who had come to cast their lot with him. Guilt touched him, for if he backed away now, he was letting them down.

But he couldn't go against Erly. His shoulders slumped. "All right, Erly. But don't you let me down a third time."

He saw triumph in the way Macy Modock relaxed, letting the rifle droop, and resentment roiled in Blair Bishop. To Greenwood he said, "You make it clear to him that I ain't givin' up, not by a damn sight. I'm just backin' off this time because you asked me to. We'll give the court a chance." His eyes narrowed. "But the court better come through right, because that's my land, and I won't stay off of it long."

He turned his horse and started back toward the herd, to bring it up to the gate as Erly had said. One of his neighbors spurred up beside him. "You don't have to call it off on our account, Blair."

"It's over with, John. At least, for today it's over with."

The neighbor frowned, looking over his shoulder toward the fence. "Then it's over for good and all. Ever give Modock a toehold, the only way you'll be shed of him is to kill him."

They brought the cattle and turned them through the gate. Blair could tell Modock had no inclination to receive them and drive them up to water, but Erly Greenwood brooked no argument, and at the moment Modock was heavily dependent upon Greenwood's reluctant backing.

Gradually the neighbors dropped out and began riding away, saying little or nothing to Blair Bishop, talking little even among themselves. Blair watched them silently, sensing the disapproval of many who had come here angry enough to fight. To them, Blair had backed down. Blair Bishop, the old warhorse, was showing his age.

It shook his self-confidence, for in his own mind he still didn't know whether he had been wrong or right. Maybe he should have gone ahead and carried through his threat. Now it was too late. The moment had come, the iron had been hot, and he had not struck. The moment might not come again.

Maybe they *were* right. Maybe Blair Bishop *was* showing his age. Maybe he should turn it over to his sons.

But he couldn't do that. Billy was not of age. And Allan was standing firm on his promise. The confrontation over and the danger past, Allan had ridden away to get

Jessie Cass.

Blair hung his head, beaten.

XI

The confrontation at the fence hadn't turned out the way Allan Bishop had expected. He had thought Blair Bishop's show of strength would have put a quick end to it, either in a volley of gunfire or by Macy Modock's capitulation in the face of heavy odds. He had really anticipated the latter, for Modock might have been vindictive and he might have been greedy, but he was not a fool. What Allan hadn't expected — and knew his father hadn't either — was Erly Greenwood's being forced to take a position that gave the decision to Modock.

Now the question remained unresolved; the problem bore on Blair Bishop heavier than ever. Allan felt a keen sense of guilt, leaving this way when it was plain his father faced deeper trouble. He knew how it would look; many would call him a quitter, deserting Blair Bishop in his hour of greatest need. Allan hadn't wanted it this way; Blair had made the ultimatum. Given any way out, Allan would have stayed and seen it through. But not at the risk of losing Jessie Cass. No telling what things were like at the Cass place anymore. Allan had made up his mind he wouldn't leave her there another day, another night.

He wished he had taken time to go to the ranch for a wagon. He figured the ranch owed him that much, for as a Bishop son he had never drawn any regular wage. But maybe now would be a good time to fetch Jessie, when Modock and his crew and Clarence Cass were occupied watering the Bishop cattle and driving them back out of the contested pasture.

Allan had no particular fear of Modock. He realized the man was reputed to be fast with a gun, and word had drifted down that Owen Darby was fast too. But Blair Bishop had always maintained and taught his sons that speed wasn't the only thing which mattered. Coolness and deliberation counted for a lot. Allan figured he had both, but he had never had occasion to test them under fire. The deliberation part told him if he could avoid a fight, he was that much better off. And getting Jessie out while everybody was gone might be a good way to sidestep trouble.

Don't run from a fight, Blair had taught his sons, but walk away right gingerly if you can.

He rode boldly up to the small, slipshod frame house that seemed to show a slight lean toward the east. West wind was pushing on it all the time, Allan thought. Somehow the whole character of Clarence Cass seemed reflected in his poor drab house.

"Jessie," he called, "you in there?"

Jessie Cass had already seen him. She ran out, almost stumbling on the wooden doorstep. He took her into his arms a moment, then released her. "You got a horse here you can ride, or have we got to ride this one double?"

Surprised, she said, "You're really takin' me away from here?"

"Told you I was."

She had been crying; he could tell by the redness of her eyes. "The fight," she asked quickly, "is it over?"

"It never started. It's a standoff of sorts, but I reckon Modock has got a little the better of it."

Her voice was bitter. "I wish somebody would kill him. If somebody doesn't, there'll be other men die."

"That's no way for a girl to be a-talkin'."

"You haven't been here. You haven't seen

him and listened to him. He's a little bit crazy, Allan."

He could tell by the way she spoke of Modock that she was afraid of him. "You won't be troubled by him no more. You got anything you need to pack, anything we can carry horseback?" He knew she didn't have much. Everything she owned could have been stuffed into a cowboy's warbag without crowding the puckerstring. Cass had never been one to spoil his daughter by teaching her vanity and a taste for worldly goods.

"I'll pack it," she said, "while you go saddle my horse for me. You'll find him grazin' down yonder in the draw, most likely."

Riding out, Allan saw a man standing in the open door of the shed, swaying. He recognized Harley Mills, once a Double B cowboy, mostly now a stable-sweeping drunk. Resentment touched Allan as he thought of Mills' falsely swearing that his homestead claim had been fraudulent.

"What're you doin' out here, Harley?" he demanded, but Mills didn't answer him and didn't have to. Allan could guess. He decided the man represented no threat to him and Jessie, so he rode on down to the draw. He found the horse, tossed a loop over its neck and led it back to the shed. Mills watched indifferently while Allan flung the sidesaddle onto the dun and led it to the house. Jessie came out carrying a faded carpetbag. "My mother's," she said. "It's about all she left me except a cheap ring and a locket."

"And the prettiest face in the country," Allan told her. He gave her a lift into the saddle. She looked around a moment, tears welling into her eyes. He asked her, "Any regrets?"

"I hate leavin' Dad. He's in trouble."

"Nothin' your stayin' could do to help him out of it." But Allan could respect her feelings, for he had the same kind himself regarding Blair Bishop.

"Where we goin'?" she asked.

"To town. I figure we'll get married there. Wouldn't be proper for us to go ridin' around all over the country together without we do the right thing first. And I got some money of my own in the bank. I thought I'd get Mister Karnes there to give me a letter of some kind so we can draw against it wherever we go. Then we'll just strike out a-lookin'. I'll find me a job on a ranch somewheres."

She said gravely, "You don't want to leave your old daddy any more than I want to leave mine."

"We got any choice?"

"I reckon not."

"Then we better be movin'. Longer we wait, the more likely we'll run into your daddy's friends."

They had already waited too long, but they didn't find out for a while. They rode side by side several miles, saying little, exchanging occasional glances but mostly keeping their own individual counsel, mulling over the intolerable conditions that had brought them to this necessity of riding away when neither really wanted to.

"Things'll work out," she said after a time. "You'll see."

He found no conviction in her voice, and there was none in his. "Sure they will."

It was on his mind that either probably would turn and go back if the other would but suggest it. Increasingly he knew he didn't want to go like this, and neither did she, leaving so much uncompleted, so much trouble still in the air. He was on the point of saying so when he saw riders coming toward them on the Cass wagon road.

Jessie gasped, "Modock!"

Allan stopped. He looked around quickly, but he saw no way to avoid the riders without running. It was contrary to all his upbringing to run. He hoped Modock still had the sheriff with him, for Erly Greenwood would see to it that there was no trouble. As the riders neared, he sagged. The sheriff must have gone back to town. Allan told Jessie, "Stay back a little. If there's a fight, I'll need room."

Clarence Cass was the first of the riders to speak after they closed the distance and stopped their horses in a crescent around Allan. He looked at his daughter in sharp surprise. "Jessie, what you doin' out here thisaway? I've told you I don't want you havin' no truck with this Bishop."

She didn't answer him. Modock spoke. "Ought to be plain enough to you, Clarence. It's plain to me. That boy yonder's a true son of his old daddy. He was fixin' to steal that little girl from you."

Allan said defiantly, "Jessie and me, we're goin' to town. We're fixin' to be married, and then we're leavin' this country."

That brought surprise even to Modock, who had never thought of the Bishops except as a cohesive unit. It hadn't occurred to him they might split away from each other in disagreement. "You meanin' to tell us you'd leave your daddy in the midst of a fight? I'm disappointed in you. You ain't a true Bishop after all. Givin' the devil his due, I'd say that Blair Bishop wouldn't never run out on *nobody*."

"I'm not runnin' out; I been *put* out. If it was up to me, I'd stay and fight you, Modock."

The tall gunman frowned, chewing quietly on something as his eyes dwelt on Allan. "Well, I'd say you got a good chance to do that right here, because I done made up my mind you ain't takin' that gal noplace."

"You got no hold on her."

Modock said, "Then I reckon I'll *put* one on her."

It came to Allan with sudden impact, a thought that had never quite reached him before. Modock had a hunger for this girl, just as Allan did. And he became certain this was as far up this road as he would get unless he could somehow beat Modock. He could see death in Modock's hard eyes.

Allan felt trapped like a fly in a spiderweb. His heart quickened. He tried to look around him without giving away his anxiety. They were moving to box him in, the red-bearded Owen Darby passing around to get behind him. But Jessie was still back a few feet, out of it. She could, if she would, spur clear. Then it would be a matter of a horse-race whether they could catch her or not. Allan said to her, "Jessie, light out of here. Don't you stop till you get to Dad. You tell him —"

Modock broke in. "She ain't fixin' to tell him nothin'. And neither are you."

Allan sensed that Jessie wouldn't do what he told her; she wouldn't run off and leave him here. He could see the intention in Modock's eyes and knew at any second Modock would reach for the pistol at his hip. He tried to remember all his father had told him about keeping his head, but none of the admonitions seemed to hold for him now. He found himself drawing inexorably toward a contest. Even as he realized he couldn't win, he found himself easing his hand down toward the butt of his pistol. *Don't be a fool,* he told himself, *they'll kill you.* But then he told himself, *They'll kill you anyhow. At least, take Modock.* He ducked low in the saddle, his hand darting for the gun.

Modock moved so swiftly Allan barely saw. He caught the swift streak of the man's pistol coming up, saw the flash and heard the explosion before his own hand had more than grasped the butt of his weapon. The bullet smashed into him like the strike of a sledge, driving him backward out of his saddle. He felt the frightened jump of his horse and felt himself suspended a moment in midair before he knew the sensation of falling. He struck the ground almost beneath his horse's hoofs.

Modock grunted. "He ducked just as I fired. I didn't get me no clean shot. But I don't reckon he'll duck again." The excited horse was in his way as he leveled the gun toward the sprawled body on the ground. Modock shouted impatiently, "Hyahhhh! Get out of here!"

Jessie Cass was on the ground, screaming at him. Before the horse galloped off in panic, clearing the way, Jessie had thrown herself over the downed boy and was looking up at Modock with eyes ablaze. "No! Don't you shoot him again."

Impatient, Modock gestured with the gun barrel. "Git aside, girl."

"I won't move. To shoot him, you'll have to shoot me first."

Owen Darby coldly rode up on the other side. "I can get him from here, Macy. She can't cover him from both of us."

Jessie Cass glanced back in desperation, knowing Darby could and would.

Clarence Cass brought himself up to mild protest. "Macy, you don't really need to do it. He's old man Blair's boy. Folks'll raise hell. You can leave when you've finished what you come to do, but me, I got to live here."

Modock flashed him a look of disgust. "Old man, you ain't ever really seen *nothin'* clear, have you? I don't figure on leavin' here at all. And I won't be finished with what I come to do till all these Bishops are put away in a pine box. This one is just the first." He turned his back on the frightened old rancher and tried to see a way to aim past Jessie without hitting her.

Jessie saw he intended to do it. She straightened, got what control she could muster and told him: "Go ahead, then, if you have to do it, but you'd better shoot me too. If you don't, I'll get you, Modock. Somewhere, somehow, I'll get hold of a gun, and I'll kill you. If I can't get a gun, I'll get a knife, and someday you'll doze off and forget to watch me, or you'll look away a minute and I'll drive that knife into you to the hilt. I'll kill you, Macy Modock. I promise, I'll kill you!"

Modock blinked, unprepared for her savage response. A chill touched him; he hadn't guessed it was in her. Yet, he could tell she meant every word, and she would carry through if it cost her life. He lowered the pistol. "Hell, maybe he'd be worth more to us alive than dead anyway. Long's we got him laid up with a bullethole bigger than a bushel basket, he won't be goin' noplace, and neither will she. Could be he'll make us a hole card if we need it to use against old Blair Bishop. Catch that horse, somebody, and we'll throw him across the saddle."

Jessie pleaded, "He'll bleed to death."

"Let him bleed. Weaker he is, the less we got to worry."

They threw him roughly up onto his horse. Jessie had used a handkerchief to help stanch the blood, and now she rode close beside him to help hold him onto the saddle. Modock glared at her.

"All right, girl, you got him. Now you better remember this. *We* got him too. First bad move you make, we'll blow him out like a lamp. You listen to every word I tell you and you do what I say. Long's you pay attention, that's how long he stays alive. Now, let's git movin'."

XII

Blair Bishop drew rein in front of the Two Forks Livery & Grain, stepped down and limped heavily into the big open door. "Harley Mills, where you at? Harley, you git yourself out here! I come to talk to you!"

He caught a shadowy movement toward the end of the horse stalls and walked angrily in that direction, cursing a little in pent-up bitterness. He slowed as an old man stepped out into view. Blair broke off the profanity. "I took you for Harley. Where the hell is he at?"

The old man shrugged. "He ain't been here in two-three days. He just up and quit his job; said he had enough money he didn't have to shovel horse manure no more. Ain't seen him since."

Blair Bishop seethed in frustration but decided this was only a momentary setback. Depending upon how much money Harley had been given, he would be either in one

149

of the saloons drinking his fill or out some-place sleeping like a man pistol-whipped. Harley was one of those bachelor cowboys who had never had a wife and didn't need one; whiskey was both his comfort and his personal hell.

"I'll find him quick enough," Bishop gritted, turning.

"I heard what he done," the old man said. "He was lyin', wasn't he?"

"He was lyin'."

"Don't think too harsh of him, Mister Blair. He can't control himself when it comes to whiskey. He'd do anything to get it."

"I don't plan to hurt him much; just bust his head if he don't tell the truth."

Followed by his son Billy, Blair tromped from one saloon to another, impatiently inquiring after Harley Mills. To his surprise, he found no one who had seen Harley in a couple of days. Harley had bought several bottles and dropped out of sight. A thought struck Blair, and he started back down the saloons, inquiring if anyone had bought any unusually large amounts of whiskey lately. At the third place, he found out Judge Quincy had bought a full case. That was strange, for Quincy was, at most, a light drinker. Whatever his shortcomings might have been, an affinity for alcohol was not one of them. His legal mind, if devious, stayed nevertheless sharp.

Blair stood outside the saloon door with young Billy, grinding his teeth. "He took Harley's deposition and then hid him out, that's what he done. He's hidin' him someplace to keep us from gettin' any chance to shake the truth out of him."

"Ain't many ranches around here would do that to you, Dad. By now they all know what Harley done. No friend of yours would help Macy Modock."

"No reason a friend of mine would have to. Ten to one they got Harley at the Cass place where Modock can keep an eye on him till he needs him in court."

"Well, then, let's go out there and git him."

Blair shook his head. "This mornin' the odds were on our side. If we was to ride out there, they'd be on Modock's side, and don't you think for a minute he wouldn't use them. He'd cut us both to pieces. And he'd have a legal leg, because we'd be the trespassers, not him."

"Then we can't touch Harley Mills?"

"Not unless he runs out of whiskey and comes to town. I'm goin' to leave word around with some friends to keep an eye out for him."

"Modock'll figure that. He won't let Harley run out of whiskey till he's through with him."

"Which only leaves Judge Quincy."

Billy grinned humorlessly and rubbed his knuckles. "Come right down to it, he's the cause of all this trouble. Without him, Modock couldn't of done a thing, hardly. Let's go work on him."

"We'll go *talk* to him," Blair corrected his eager son. "And I'll do all the talkin'."

The moment Blair Bishop's shadow fell across his door Quincy was on his feet. He hurried behind a long table spread with papers and law books and turned defensively. "Blair Bishop, I been promised the sheriff's protection. You lay one hand on me and I'll sue you for every acre you got, every cow . . ."

"Settle down, Judge." Blair's voice was dry. "I come friendly. No, I take that back . . . not friendly. But I come peaceful. All I want to do is talk."

"We've done our talking. Anything else you have to say to me you can say it in court."

Blair eyed him thoughtfully. "I ain't no lawyer, Judge, but through the years I've picked up a legal word here and there. One of them is *perjury.* Another is *disbarment.*"

"You'll not get away with threatening me. Intimidation is against the law . . ."

"I ain't threatenin', and I ain't intimidatin'. Let's say I'm askin' for a little bit of legal information, and I'm willin' to pay the goin' fee for it. My question is this: how does a man go about filin' for disbarment of a lawyer who knowingly builds up a case based on perjury . . . who maybe even personally bribes a witness to give false testimony?"

"You're still trying to intimidate a legally licensed attorney into defaulting on a client, Blair Bishop. The bar will not hold still for it."

"I never mentioned your name; never mentioned nobody's name. I just asked for a piece of legal information. If you don't care to answer it, I can go to somebody else who knows law. Maybe the district judge . . ."

Blair's leg hurt; he'd slept little, and he had done a lot of riding. He shifted his weight. Quincy took that for a move forward, and he cringed. "Bishop, don't you come any closer. I have a gun in here. I'll use it."

Blair heard footsteps scrape across the threshold, and he saw relief flush over Quincy's face. Quincy said, "Sheriff, you sure took your time getting here."

Blair glanced back at Erly Greenwood. "Howdy, Erly. Seems like a man runs into you almost everyplace these days, except when he needs you."

"Maybe you do need me right now, Blair. Maybe you was about to do somethin' that could cost you more than you could afford to pay."

"I wasn't goin' to do anything to him. I'm as close right now as I ever care to be. The smell of him would kill cotton at forty paces."

Erly studied Blair Bishop gravely. "Blair, you got trouble enough without makin' it worse. Why don't you go on home and get some sleep? Then maybe you'll be in a better position to think things through. Better yet, you come on over to my house and bunk down awhile. You'll see things clearer."

"I'm tired, but I ain't blind. I see things clear enough. Quincy bribed Harley Mills into makin' a deposition that he homesteaded his place through fraud and that I was the one put him up to it, so I could buy the land from him. You know it's a lie; Quincy knows it's a lie. But some visitin' judge from another part of the state won't know it's a lie unless Harley or Quincy owns up to it. I come to talk sense to Quincy."

"And I come to talk sense to you, Blair. A mistake right now could cost you your case."

"I ain't fixin' to lose my land, Erly, not to a set of lies told by a crooked lawyer and a whiskey-soaked stable sweeper."

"You *could* lose it. You got to walk easy till this thing has come to a head. You got to keep your distance from Judge Quincy. It's my job to give him protection."

"Seems to me like you been takin' your job awful seriously here of late."

"I always did, Blair." Erly shook his head, taking a hard, long look at Quincy. "And there's never been a time I ever hated it till now."

Quincy watched the sheriff until he found confidence in himself. "You're letting your personal feelings influence you, Greenwood. A peace officer cannot afford to do that."

"A peace officer cannot afford to let his personal feelings be an influence in what he does," Erly corrected him. "There's no law can keep an officer from havin' them. You know mine. Somethin' for you to keep in mind if ever I catch you steppin' over the line."

The sheriff followed Blair and Billy out into the street. Blair stood slumped, exhausted in body and spirit. "Seems like every way I turn, they got me boxed, Erly."

"I'm sorry they've made me a party to it. Only way I could change it would be to resign, and that wouldn't help anything. The next man couldn't do no different, not and live up to his oath."

"Don't resign, Erly. Maybe they'll make a mistake. Then we'll need you behind that badge."

"And if they don't make any mistakes?"

Blair thought awhile. "Then I'll need you to keep me from makin' one and killin' them all."

Erly walked along with him. He didn't have to move very fast, for Blair was dragging some. He said, "Blair, I still wish you'd come out to the house and rest awhile. You need it."

"I got a lot of thinkin' to do. I think better at home." It occurred to him to ask, "You never have found any sign of Joe Little?"

Erly shook his head. "None at all. He's plumb left the country."

"I don't agree with you. I still believe he was the first mistake Macy Modock made."

"You keep thinkin' that, Blair, if it'll make you feel any better."

"It don't help my feelin'. But it helps keep me convinced that one way or another, I got to stop Macy Modock. Only thing bothers me is, how many more men will he kill before I get *him?*"

Harley Mills was well into his second bottle for the day, but his vision wasn't so foggy he couldn't see that one of the horses was bringing somebody wounded. The thought filtered through his brain that he could've told them old Blair Bishop would fight like a mountain lion with its tail in a steel trap, that they wouldn't come home in one piece. But they hadn't asked him. They hadn't asked him much of anything, come to think of it.

Well, it wasn't going to be any bother to him one way or the other. The hell with them. Soon as they got that court hearing over with and paid him off, Harley Mills was going to be long gone out of this country. He didn't give a damn then if Modock and all of his bunch got shot into pieces too little for chili. In fact, he almost hoped they would. He found it impossible ever to feel easy in the presence of Modock or Owen Darby. He never got over the feeling that Darby would shoot a man just for the fun of seeing him jump and fall, and that Modock had some devil chewing on him all the time. Mills would be glad to get the money in his hands and run. It had occurred to him more than once that for the amount promised him, Modock probably wouldn't hesitate to kill a man.

I'll be sober that day, Mills pledged himself, *and I'll have eyes in the back of my head. Once I get paid off, all they'll see of Harley Mills is a blue streak and a little cloud of dust.*

He didn't care enough to get up and go see who was wounded; he didn't know any of these Modock men anyway, and if it was old man Clarence the world would be that much better off, in Mills' view. But his interest was aroused a little when he saw Cass' girl, Jessie, jump down from her sidesaddle. The way he had seen her ride away from here earlier with that young Bishop, he had figured she was gone for good. Mills blinked as they led the wounded man's horse up to the shed where he lay with the bottle. To his surprise he recognized Allan Bishop. Mills staggered to his feet, stumbled over a pitchfork and got up again. His first thought was, *He'll tell old Blair where I'm at and he'll come after me with a bullwhip or a gun.* Then he realized that the shape Allan appeared to be in, he wouldn't be going anywhere. Mills tried to figure out how come they had brought young Bishop here, but liquor had left him no chance with logic. Nothing came very clear to him except that an uncomfortable situation was becoming increasingly bad.

"Move over, Mills," Macy Modock said curtly. "We got to have that cot you been lyin' on."

Mills stared in confusion at the unconscious Allan Bishop. "How come him to be here?" He was too puzzled even to feel resentment over being done out of his cot. He would have to sleep on the hay now.

"We shot him," Modock said.

"Old man Blair'll come huntin' him, and there'll be hell to pay."

"Bishop figures he run off with the Cass girl," Modock said. "He won't be lookin' for him."

Mills stared down at the blood-streaked face. "He goin' to die?" He had punched cows with Allan, back when Allan was just a kid. He had been a good-enough kind of a button, Mills had always thought, considering that he was the son of a big cowman like Blair Bishop. A little humility wouldn't have hurt him none, but Mills wouldn't have wished him a bullet. "Somebody better fetch him a doctor."

"No doctor," said Modock. "The less Blair Bishop knows, the better. I'll tell him myself if I think the time is right."

"What if that boy was to die?"

"Then I'd give you a shovel and tell you

to go bury him, since you're a friend of his. And if you said a word to anybody about it, I'd see that you was buried right next to him. Do you get that through your head, Mills?"

Harley nodded, fearing the man. But he had another fear too. "If Blair finds out about this, I sure don't want him thinkin' I had anything to do with it."

Modock snarled. "You and old Clarence . . . neither one of you has got sense enough to see daylight. Time I get through, Blair Bishop won't trouble *nobody*."

Harley Mills sat on the ground and silently pulled at the bottle as he watched tearful Jessie Cass and her father dig the bullet out of Allan and wrap clean cloth around the wound. He listened to Clarence Cass complaining. "I didn't noways figure on nothin' like this. I ain't a-goin' to stand for it. One of these days I'm goin' to walk up to Macy Modock and I'm goin' to tell him . . ."

Mills snorted to himself, feeling better in the knowledge that he wasn't the only coward on the place. *You ain't goin' to tell him nothin', Clarence, same as I ain't goin' to tell him nothin'. You're goin' to listen and say yes, sir. Difference is, I'm goin' to get my money and ride out of here. What're you goin' to get, Clarence?*

XIII

Blair Bishop lay down for a fitful nap when he got home, but he arose for a supper quickly cooked by Chaco Martinez. Mostly he drank coffee. It didn't make him feel any easier, but it woke him up. He stayed awake long past his accustomed bedtime, bolstered by a notion that Allan would get over his anger and come on home. He didn't really believe his son would leave here at a time like this, angry or not. And Blair had cooled too, in the face of so many other problems. He could remember how strongly the tides of young manhood had surged in him when he was Allan's age and could, now that he was calmer, understand why the boy would turn his back on father and home in favor of a girl. Blair sat on the porch a long time, sometimes rocking, sometimes still, listening vainly for hoofbeats. He fell asleep finally and woke up with a crick in his neck. Sadly he made his way to bed, knowing Allan wasn't coming.

Next morning he was up early, problems still unresolved. He knew what he had to do about one of them, and he had to do it quick. He had to get a lot of cattle off of his land in a hurry or he wouldn't have anything left except their sun-whitened bones.

He ate his breakfast at the bunkhouse with the men. "Bad as I hate to," he told them, "we got to take a deep cut into the cow herd. We can't sell them at home. It's so dry that most people here are more of a mind to sell than to buy. We'll make a drag on our oldest cows and drive them over to the railroad. Maybe we can get a decent price for them in Kansas City."

Billy Blair put in, "Seems like an awful pity to have to sell off them good Double B cows."

"Be a worse pity to watch them die for water. If we can save the young cows, we'll at least have seed."

"There was a time," Billy said, "when you wouldn't have done it this way. You'd have took care of Macy Modock and everything would've been all right."

Blair frowned. It surprised him, the quick-fighting spirit Billy was showing these days. Blair wondered where his son had gotten this sudden contrariness from; certainly not from his father. "Times change, boy. There was a time years ago when I could've killed Modock and nobody would've said a word."

"You sorry now you didn't?"

Blair thought about it a minute. "Maybe. For some things in this world, there's no cure as dependable as a good old-fashioned funeral."

He took the small crew to the Black Bull pasture where yesterday's trouble had been. There the water problem was most immediate, and most acute. The cattle had been watered yesterday. Today there wouldn't be enough. The cowboys made a broad sweep of the pasture, pushing all the cattle before them. As they moved, Blair Bishop rode back and forth among them, cutting out the younger cows carefully as he could without disrupting the herd. No use walking them extra miles for nothing. He kept the big steers in the herd, and the older cows, and the steer calves and yearlings. These were expendable. These would walk the better part of two days to the railroad.

When he had finished cutting the herd, Blair looked back for sign of Chaco Martinez. He had told Chaco to load the chuck wagon and bring it, for cowboys had to eat along the trail. They had to have changes of horses, too. He sent Hez Northcutt to round up the remuda. Then Blair took the point and let Billy and the rest of the riders string the herd out behind him. Some of the cattle were bawling, for they already had walked miles in the roundup and were showing thirst. They would have to skirt around Clarence Cass' land, for they would find no welcome there, Blair knew. But beyond Clarence lay the Finley ranch, and John Finley would spare water for a neighbor's passing herd as long as a drop was left.

They walked the cattle through the heat of the afternoon, thirst cracking Blair's dry lips as he rode along watching the dancing dust devils and peering toward the shimmering horizon line that changed but slowly in the deliberate pace of the herd. Chaco rode ahead and off to the right, keeping the wagon out of the herd's dust, for cowboys who ate dust all day didn't want to find it in their supper at night. Along late in the afternoon Blair called Billy up to take his place on the point and loped ahead to find John Finley and get permission to water the herd.

Blair's conscience hurt him as he watched his cattle watering by twilight, the stronger cows hooking impatiently at the weaker ones, fighting their way down to the deeper water. John had only a surface tank, much like Blair's own Black Bull Tank had been. When it emptied, that would be all of it until rain came again. But John hadn't had the heart to turn down Blair Bishop in his time of trouble. Blair shouted at the men, "Let's keep them movin'. Let them get enough water, but don't let them stay too long." Normally he would have bedded the cattle for the night near water, but this was not a normal situation. Soon as they had slaked their thirst, Blair moved out on point and had the cowboys push them a couple more miles to get them away from John's dwindling tank. Maybe they hadn't had all the water they wanted, but they had had enough to see them through another day's drive. There would be water again at the railroad.

The cowboys strung the cattle out in the cool of the morning and walked them steadily, pushing for all the miles they could get without hurting the stock. As the day wore on and the heat came up, the cattle slowed, bawling in distress. Blair plodded along, matching his pace to that of the cattle. He had water in a canteen, but he used it sparingly. Somehow it didn't seem right for a man to drink when his stock was suffering. Blair rode steadily and suffered with them.

Sometime after noon he began noticing the clouds change. Up to then, they had been the same puffy white clouds he had watched drift aimlessly across the sky all the dry spring and summer, leaving no benefit other than a brief respite from the sun's burning heat as they passed over the land. Now, however, the clouds seemed to thicken and turn darker.

Could it be that a summertime rain was coming up? Blair felt his pulse quicken a little at the thought. It wasn't often that a drought broke in this country in August, but sometimes a man got lucky and caught enough hard, pounding rain to run the draws and fill his tanks, to revive the grass and keep its roots alive until the more generous fall rains gave it one last chance before winter.

As the clouds became a leaden gray in the north, excitement built in Blair Bishop. He was tempted to stop the herd. If it would just come one of those old-timey chip floaters and fill his tanks, his cattle would have water enough. He wouldn't have to sell them.

But he knew that since he had gone this far, he had as well go the whole way to the railroad. The grass would revive better and the land would hair over sooner if he got some of the excess cattle off of it.

Riding point, he came to the creekbed where a flash flood had swept the cowboy named Abernathy to his death years ago. The creek was bone dry, as Blair had known it would be. Watching the clouds, he had a feeling it was a good thing the crew would have time enough to get the herd across before the rain started.

He was tired, and he was still desperately thirsty, but it didn't bother him now. He didn't seem to feel it. All he could feel was a faintly cooler wind coming out of the north, out from under those beautiful clouds. *Any minute now, she's going to start,* he thought. *Any minute now, we're goin' to get ourselves soaked.*

A drop of water struck his hat brim, and he turned his face up to the sky. A couple more drops splattered across his nose and his mouth. He turned in the saddle and gave a loud holler that would carry all the way to the drag end of the herd.

But something happened. Even as he watched, the cloud began to split almost directly overhead. He could see blue sky through a rift. As quickly as they had made up, the clouds broke apart and began drifting away. Blair watched dry-mouthed and stunned.

He had seen clouds break up like this more times than he could ever count. But he had never seen a time he had so desperately wanted it to rain.

The sun broke through, as hot as it had ever been. Blair pulled his hat down low to protect his eyes from it. His eyes were burning a little, somehow; must have gotten dust in them. His throat was tight. All of a sudden he realized anew how thirsty he was, and how far it still was to the railroad. He slumped in the saddle and rode along in silent misery.

Late in the afternoon he summoned Billy. "Looks to me like we ought to make it to the shippin' pens about dark. I was thinkin' me and you would ride in and make arrangements with the agent for water and hay. Ain't likely they can spot cars for us till tomorrow sometime."

Billy nodded and went back with orders for someone else to take the point. Then he reined in beside his father, his dusty face proud. This was a sign he was coming of age; this was the sharing of a man's job. Any kid could drive cattle; it took somebody responsible to handle the business end of a ranch.

Blair studied his youngest son as they rode and he liked what he saw. Give the boy a couple-three more years and he would be the man Allan was. Maybe if Blair was lucky, Billy wouldn't fall in love with the wrong woman, either. Time had come, Blair guessed, to talk to him straight-out about things like responsibility, and women and such as that. Maybe that had been the trouble with Allan; maybe Blair hadn't talked to him enough.

I won't make that mistake with Billy, Blair thought. *I'll sure talk to him. But not today; I'm too dry. I'll get around to it one of these days, when the right time comes.*

Blair saw dust rising from the railroad shipping pens and knew another herd was there ahead of him. Late as it was already, he figured it unlikely that herd would load out tonight.

"That's too bad," he said. "I'd figured we could turn them cattle into the pens on hay and water. Then we wouldn't have to fool with them."

Curiosity would normally have carried him by the pens to look at the cattle, but he had too much on his mind now to spend time on idle things. He rode straight to the depot. Every bone in him ached as he handed his reins to Billy and limped up the plank steps. Billy tied the horses and followed him. First thing Blair did was to find the water bucket and empty the dipper three times . . . twice down his throat and once over his head. Handing it to Billy, he turned and sought the railroad agent. The agent was a fairly new man, for Blair didn't recognize him. He said, "I got a herd of cattle comin' in directly. Blair Bishop, from over at Two Forks. Need cars to take them to Kansas City. Tonight we'll need hay and water."

The agent explained what Blair had already seen, that another herd had preceded him and had occupied the corrals. "However, we have a large water lot with troughs in it. You can bring the cattle, water them good, then take them back out and herd them on the prairie till the train comes tomorrow."

"That'll have to do," Blair said. The agent sat down and began filling out the papers. "Bishop," he murmured. "Blair Bishop. I believe I've shipped cattle for you before, Mister Bishop. What's that brand again?"

"A Double B."

The agent looked up in surprise. "Perhaps I misunderstood you, Mister Blair. You talked as if your cattle were still to come in."

"They are. They'll be here in an hour, give or take a little."

"But most of those cattle down there waiting for shipment are Double B too. Let me see." He riffled through a sheaf of papers and came up with one. "Yes, it says right here: Double B. Bishop ranch. They were signed for by one of your cowboys."

Blair looked incredulously at Billy, then back at the agent. He reached for the paper. "Let me have a look at that." His gaze went quickly down the paper till he reached the signature at the bottom. "That's no cowboy of mine. I never heard of this man."

The agent blinked. "But those cattle carry your brand, and your name . . ." He stood up solemnly. "We've got a deputy sheriff here. I think I'd better get him."

Blair nodded, suddenly grim. "I think you'd better. We'll go with you."

They found the deputy relaxed in the shade at a livery barn. This was a different county than Erly Greenwood's, and Blair didn't know the lawman. But he thought by the look in the man's eyes that he probably savvied his line of work, for he had a riot-stopping stare. The deputy had heard of Blair Bishop. He shook hands. "My name's Hawk. Family name. Folks around here nicknamed me Bird. I'd still rather it was Hawk."

"Hawk," Blair said, "the agent tells me there's cattle in them shippin' pens carryin' my brand. There oughtn't to be. I'd like you to go with me to investigate."

The deputy was immediately all business. "I'll saddle my old pony and be right with you."

It didn't take him a minute. Blair turned to his son. "Billy, if I'd had any thought of trouble, I wouldn't of brought you. I want you to stay here."

Billy's reply wasn't argumentative; it was a plain statement of fact. "Like hell I will. I stayed home the last time."

Momentarily inclined to raise Cain with him, Blair decided against it. At Billy's age he had taken on all of a man's responsibilities and was the veteran of two Indian fights. "All right, boy, but you watch yourself."

They rode to the shipping pens in an easy trot. Blair took the shotgun out of his scabbard, painfully loaded it with an aching hand and laid it across his lap to be ready. Hawk eyed him warily. "Mister Bishop, we'll talk first."

"That," Blair said, "depends on them."

Two cowboys were in a corral spreading

172

hay. Blair needed only a glance to know that the cattle in the pen were his. They carried the Double B and his earmark. He told the deputy so.

The deputy said, "I know them two hands, Mister Bishop. They been around town here lookin' for work. I didn't figure them for thieves."

"Can't always tell by looks. Damn few cow rustlers go around carryin' a sign."

Without dismounting, the deputy hailed the two cowboys over to the fence. They came without apparent suspicion, until they spotted Blair's shotgun casually aimed in their direction. That stopped them in consternation. "Boys," the deputy spoke, "we come to talk to you. We want to know whose cows them are yonder."

One of the cowboys moved up cautiously, his eyes never leaving the shotgun. "They belong to a feller name of Bishop. Lives over at Two Forks."

The deputy asked, "Do you know Bishop?"

"No, sir, never met him."

Blair demanded, "Then what're you doin' with them cows?"

"We was hired to help drive them up here and see they got shipped all right."

Blair eased off with the shotgun, for he

began to suspect these men were the inevitable innocent bystanders who get hurt in every fight. "Who hired you?"

"His foreman. Leastways, he said he was." The two cowboys were beginning to sense the way the wind blew. "Said he'd pay us ten dollars apiece to help make the drive and stay till the shippin' was done."

"He paid you yet?" Blair asked.

"Not yet."

"Then you've likely lost ten dollars apiece. I'm Blair Bishop."

The cowboys gave each other a sick look. One of them tried a weak smile that didn't work. "Somehow, I was startin' to suspect that. Last we seen of that foreman, him and a pal of his was over in the Legal Tender havin' a snort and waitin' for the train."

The deputy motioned. "You-all come with us. You'll have to point them out."

The cowboys were eager, for by now nobody had to explain the situation any further to them. They might come out of this broke, but they wanted to be sure they came out of it clean. There had been a time not too long before when a man caught with somebody else's cattle stood a good chance of looking up a rope at a nice, sturdy tree limb. Climbing into his saddle, one of the cowboys studied Blair the way a jackrabbit might study a wolf. "Mister Bishop, I bet you ain't even *got* a foreman." Blair said, "I did have. He was killed."

The cowboy pleaded, "We didn't know. We needed work, and we took him for what he said he was. We sure don't want no trouble."

Blair said, "You just point him out, and you won't be in no trouble."

They reined up a few doors from the Legal Tender and went on afoot. All but Billy. Blair told him to ride around to the back door. If anybody came running out, Billy was to detain him. Blair figured it would be much safer out there than in the saloon.

The front doors stood wide open, and all the windows were up, for the heat still lingered here into the dusk. The cowboys walked in front of Blair and the deputy. They paused at the door. One pointed. "That's him, the one yonder with the ventilation holes punched in his hat." Blair squinted. Two men sat at a small table, a bottle half emptied in front of them. They had both been with Macy Modock at the Harley Mills fence.

He realized he had never thought to count the cattle Modock had pushed out of that pasture. Other things had seemed far more important at the time. Now he knew Mo-dock had probably shorted him, depending upon there being no count. And he realized where some of the other cattle he had been missing must have gone.

The cowboys stepped back out of the way. Blair moved into the saloon, flanked by the deputy. The two men looked up. Recognition was instantaneous. Both jumped to their feet.

Other men in the saloon dived for cover as the one who had posed as foreman whipped a pistol out of his waistband, his eyes on Blair. *He'll take me first,* Blair thought, bringing the shotgun up into line and stiff-handedly pulling the trigger. Even as the weapon boomed, he knew he had jerked too hard and had missed. But the re-action to the blast threw off the cow thief's aim. His shot went astray. He never got a chance for a second one. The deputy's pistol roared, and the man staggered back.

The second man never made a move toward his pistol. He ran for the open back door. Blair leveled the shotgun at him, but he had no time to reload. The deputy was too engrossed in seeing that the first man didn't fire again to do more than glance at the second. The man hit the door in a dead run.

Blair heard Billy cry out for him to stop. Shots were fired, and Blair could hear horses' hoofs as he limped toward the door, feverishly trying to reload the shotgun and fumbling it. He hit the back step and saw Billy Blair running toward a fallen man. A horse galloped away in panic, stirrups flopping.

Billy stood over the man, smoking pistol in his hand. Blair rushed to him, followed by the deputy and the two cowboys. Other men from the saloon trailed in curiosity.

The deputy looked at the man, who lay sprawled on his stomach. He turned him over, puzzled. "Where'd you hit him, son?"

"I didn't," Billy said, barely above a whisper. "I missed him." He trembled from shock. "He grabbed a horse and tried to run off. He was lookin' back at me. He didn't see that clothesline."

The deputy felt for a pulse, then laid his ear to the man's chest. "You can tell by the way his head lays that he broke his neck. See that rope burn? Done the same as if he'd dropped through a trapdoor with a hemp necktie on."

Blair Bishop placed his hand on Billy's shoulder. "Good thing it turned out this way, boy. You're a shade too young to have a man on your conscience."

"In a way," Billy said regretfully, "I did do it."

"He wasn't runnin' from you, really. He was runnin' from a hangrope. He missed one and found another." Blair turned back to the deputy. "The other one . . . he dead too?"

The deputy nodded. "Been a poor day for cow thieves."

Bishop scowled. "And for me too. I wish we could've got them alive . . . one of them, anyway. Now we got no way to prove Macy Modock was behind them. Far as any court can tell, they was workin' for themselves."

He had explained a little about Modock to the deputy as they had ridden in from the shipping pens. The deputy shook his head sympathetically. "Sorry, Mister Bishop."

"Can't be helped. At least we all still got our health." He rubbed his hurting hand. "Most of it, anyway."

The deputy said, "I reckon now you'll want to claim your cattle."

Blair nodded. "Long as they're already here, I'd just as well ship them with the others I got comin' in. No point in drivin' them back to a dried-out range." He turned to the two cowboys. "You said they promised you ten dollars apiece. I got a herd out yonder. I'll pay you ten dollars if you'll meet them and help bring them on in."

"Fair enough, Mister Bishop." The cowboys rode off in the direction Blair pointed, glad they hadn't found themselves neck deep in trouble.

Blair and Billy rode to the pens again. Blair sat outside the fence on his horse, looking across at some young heifers he wished he could save. Billy rode on around to look at the rest of the cattle. Presently he came back. "Dad," he said urgently, "these ain't all yours."

Blair was a little surprised, though he realized he shouldn't be. A cow thief was not likely to be particular. "Whose are the rest of them?"

"There's a bunch of C Bars in there, too. Clarence Cass."

That *did* surprise Blair, till he had time to think about it a little. Gradually, though, it all began to fit. He laughed dryly when the full irony of the situation came to him. Cass was offering sanctuary to Macy Modock, hoping to see Modock break Blair Bishop, and all the time Modock was stealing from the old man too.

"Cast thy bread upon the waters . . ." Blair Bishop mused. "I reckon old Clarence's bread must've been a little moldy."

XIV

Macy Modock was napping out the afternoon heat when Owen Darby gripped his shoulder and shook him. "Somebody's comin' yonder," Darby said. "Can't tell yet who it is, but I'm pretty sure it ain't Jim and Charlie back from the railroad."

Macy Modock got to his feet and wiped the sweat from his face. He strode out into the yard, softly cursing the interruption and looking down the wagon road. Recognition was slow in coming, but when it came he was suddenly wide awake. "It's Blair Bishop. And he's got the sheriff with him." Modock turned quickly, barking orders. "Owen, you put one of the boys out in the shed to watch that girl and the Bishop boy. No . . . come to think of it . . . you better do it yourself. Tell that girl if she makes as much as a howdydo you'll blow that boy's brains out. And keep Harley Mills out of sight too. Old Bishop'd just love to see him here."

Darby strode to the nearby shed. The rest of Modock's tough crew strayed up from one place and another. Clarence Cass shuffled out of the house sleepy-eyed. "What's goin' on?"

Modock spat, "You just stand back and keep your mouth shut, Clarence. One wrong word and I'll bust out what few teeth you still got left."

Cass stood blinking, trying to figure what he had said wrong.

Modock didn't trust even Darby to do a job without supervision. He looked into the shed. He found Harley Mills seated on the hay-strewn floor, his back to the wall, a near-empty bottle in his hands and an empty look in his eyes. Allan Bishop lay in a fever, half out of his head. The girl sat in a rawhide chair beside the cot, placing wet cloths over Allan's face every now and then. Her eyes hated Modock as she looked up. Owen Darby stood with his back to the wall, pistol pointed at Allan.

"I told her like you said, Macy. If they see her, or hear a sound out of this shed, the boy's dead." Argument showed in his eyes. "But hell, Macy, there ain't but the two of them. You been wantin' to kill Blair Bishop all this time. It'd be easy now."

"Too quick. I ain't got him to his knees

yet. Anyway, we'd have to kill the sheriff too. I don't want to run no more. I want to do this in a way that when it's over, I can stay here and enjoy what I've got." He looked at Jessie.

Darby shrugged. "However you want it, Macy. Just seems to me sometimes like you sure go about things the hard way."

"But it's my way. Don't you mess it up."

Modock checked his pistol to be sure it was fully loaded, then walked out into the yard. He didn't plan to use it, but a man never could tell. He stood waiting beside a nervous Clarence Cass while the sheriff and Blair Bishop took their own sweet time about riding in.

The sheriff spoke first. "Howdy, Clarence. Modock."

Blair Bishop looked at Modock, but he spoke to Cass. "Clarence."

Ranch country custom called for a man to invite any visitor to light and hitch, whether he be friend or enemy. But Modock had never been one to concern himself over any custom but his own. "Sheriff, you're welcome here any time." He pointedly left out Bishop.

Blair Bishop observed with a touch of sarcasm, "I'd always thought this was Clarence Cass' place." He glanced at Cass in a way that was like rubbing salt into an open sore.

"Me and Clarence is partners," Modock said.

Bishop grunted. "I'm glad to hear that. I thought you'd taken plumb over." He was still looking at Cass, making sure the point wasn't lost. It wasn't.

Modock growled, "You didn't come over here to say howdy."

The sheriff shook his head. "No, we didn't." He looked at the men gathered loosely around Modock. "Seems to me like you had a couple or three more men when you throwed Blair's cattle out of that pasture."

Suspiciously Modock said, "A couple. Does that make any difference?"

Blair Bishop braced his hands against the saddle horn and leaned forward, shifting his weight to one side to ease an aching leg. "We was over at the railroad yesterday. Drove a bunch of cattle there to ship. We found another herd had got there ahead of us. Funny thing about them cattle. Big part of them was wearin' the Double B brand."

Modock frowned. "I wouldn't know nothin' about that."

"There was a couple of your friends over there with them. One was shippin' the cattle and signin' himself as a sales agent for me. The money was supposed to come back to him."

The sheriff said, "To've got them cattle to the railroad yesterday, they had to be gone from here two or three days. Don't a thing like that make you suspicious, Modock?"

"A couple of my boys quit me after that set-to over at the fence. They was nervous about all them guns. Maybe they decided to take a little somethin' with them as they went."

"Maybe so," said Bishop. "Now, Macy, you'll be glad to know that the money for them cattle will all come to me."

"Always tickled to see the right thing done." Modock's dark eyes were a-glitter with anger. "What did you do with them two boys?"

The sheriff said, "They're buryin' them today."

Modock's eyes momentarily flashed a fury he was helpless to hide. He had figured on that money . . . had counted on getting it. Losing it threw a monkey wrench into a bunch of things, but he said, "I reckon they had it comin'. If there's anything I got no use for, it's a thief."

Bishop glanced at the sheriff. "Well, Erly, since Macy wasn't noway involved, I reckon we got no more business here." He started to pull away, then looked at Clarence Cass. "Clarence, I was wonderin' about that daughter of yours. I don't see her noplace around."

Cass shook his head, trembling. "No, you don't."

Bishop nodded solemnly. "Then I take it she's gone. My boy Allan, he said he was goin' to come get her. I hoped maybe he'd come to his senses." Bishop showed disappointment, and he looked a moment at the ground. Then he brought his gaze back to Cass. "One other thing, Clarence. You took any count on your cattle lately?"

Cass' mouth came open in puzzlement. "No, why?"

"Because all them cattle over at the railroad wasn't mine. A big bunch of them was yours." Bishop paused, watching an explosive reaction in Cass' whiskered face. "Since they was already in the shippin' pens and since you're overstocked anyway, I told the station agent to go ahead and load them out for Kansas City along with mine. The payment will come to you."

Clarence Cass' face was flushed. He looked sharply at Modock, then away. Bishop added with an evident touch of malice, "The station agent told me them wasn't the first of your cattle *or* mine that've been shipped lately. Been several other loads gone out. Naturally my first thought was that Macy Modock done it. But from what he tells us, I guess he didn't . . . seein' as you're such good partners." His voice went bitter. "Surely Macy wouldn't have no call to be stealin' from himself." Bishop pulled his horse away. "*Adiós,* Clarence."

Clarence Cass seethed, and Modock knew it, but he didn't give a damn. He stood simmering in his own frustration over loss of that herd, and over the fact that Bishop and the sheriff were wise to him, even if they lacked evidence to make a legal move. He would have the devil's own time getting any more Bishop cattle out from under old Blair's nose. And Modock wanted that money.

Owen Darby walked over from the shed, squinting after the departing riders and making it plain he had rather have seen them lying here on the ground. "How come Bishop to bring the sheriff, since he didn't make no move against us?"

"Protection. Knew we wouldn't do nothin' long as the sheriff was here."

"But I don't see what he come for in the first place."

"Sniffin'. He's an old bloodhound, that

Bishop. Lookin' for that boy of his, for one thing. Lookin' for anything he might be able to use against us. And lookin' for a chance to stir up trouble between us and Clarence."

Cass could contain himself no longer. "You been stealin' from me, Macy. We made a deal, and then you turned around and went to takin' my cattle."

"Shut up, Clarence."

"Damn you, Macy . . ." Cass' fury had momentarily overcome his fear. "Damn you for a double-crossin' thief!"

Modock's short fuse went up in smoke. He brought his fist around and struck the old man square in the face, hitting him so hard that Clarence went down on his back. Nose bloodied, the rancher raised up onto one elbow. "Damn you all to hell, Macy! I'm goin' to ride after the sheriff and tell him . . ."

Modock reached down and grabbed Cass' shirtfront, savagely hauling the old man to his feet and striking him down again. His voice dropped to almost a whisper — a deadly one. "If I thought you would — If I thought there was even a chance you would do that, Clarence, I'd wring your scrawny neck the way I'd kill a rooster."

Cass tried to crawl away, and Modock

kicked him hard enough to have caved in his ribs if he had hit him right. "But you ain't goin' to do it, old man. You got too much blood on your own hands. You ain't goin' to say a word . . . not one little bitty word. You was there when we killed Joe Little. You was with us when we broke into the bank to make it look like he done it and ran off."

"You forced me to go with you to the bank. And I didn't have nothin' to do with that killin'. You-all done it."

"You was there. You was an accessory. The court that hangs us hangs *you*. So you'll keep your mouth shut, Clarence, or I'll shut it for you. And when I shut it, it'll stay shut for good." He grabbed the old man again and pulled him up, taking such a grip on the shirtfront that Clarence nearly choked. "Anything you don't understand, Clarence?"

The old man sobbed in fear. "No, Macy, no."

Macy dropped him. Clarence lay on the ground at Modock's feet. Modock's anger led him to say the rest of it. "Sure, we was stealin' your cattle. You was too lazy to get out and look, and too stupid to've seen if you'd been out. I was goin' to steal you blind and buy you out with the money from your own cattle. I already had Judge Quincy draw up the papers for you to sign when the time come. You'd of took your money and left this country, and this ranch would be mine. This ranch first, then Blair Bishop's. And all the people that stood around and rubbed their hands when Macy Modock went to prison, I'd have them sweatin' blood."

Cass murmured, "Blair Bishop'll stop you now."

"There ain't nobody stoppin' me. I was goin' to pay you for this ranch, but now I'll have it without payin' you, Clarence. You'll sign them papers for nothin'. You'll sign them because you know I'll kill you if you don't."

"This ranch is all I got."

"Not anymore it ain't. I'm takin' it."

"But what'll me and Jessie do? Take this away and we got nothin'."

"I'm takin' Jessie away from you too, old man. I been wantin' her since the first day I ever seen her. I've held off with her till I could have it all. Now I'm *takin'* it all." He leaned down. "Get up, Clarence. You got papers to sign."

The old man wept. "You'll kill me when I do."

"I'll kill you if you don't."

"I won't sign them, Macy. I won't sign them."

Modock hauled him to his feet. "You will. I'll put you out in that shed and let you look at that Bishop boy awhile. You figure how you'd like to be in the shape he is. You'll sign." Modock shoved him toward the shed. The old man stumbled and went to his knees. Roughly Modock picked him up and shoved him again. "Git in there, Clarence. You'll git in there till you've made up your mind. I ain't foolin' with you no more; I ain't goin' to soft-talk with you. I'll come in ever' so often and stomp on you a little bit to help make up your mind."

In the shed, Modock looked a moment at the girl, and he felt a strong urge to grab her by the hand and drag her over to the house. But he would wait; she wouldn't try to go anywhere as long as that Bishop boy was there and helpless. Taking her now might cause old Clarence to do something foolish and not ever get around to signing those papers. Moreover, he still had Harley Mills here, and he depended upon Mills' testimony to help him wrest that land away from Blair Bishop. Mills was a man of no particular character, but even a bottle bum might climb out over the fence if he saw Modock use force on the girl.

"Keep an eye on them, Owen," Modock said to Darby. "Old Clarence has got some thinkin' to do."

Darby nodded. "Want me to help him?"

"I'll take care of that, Owen. You might overdo things, and a dead man don't write very good."

Clarence Cass withered up into a huddle of misery. He sat hunched on the floor, tears running down his cheeks and into his beard, his thin shoulders shaking as he wept in helplessness.

Jessie looked at him in a mixture of disappointment and pity. "You're dead if you sign them papers."

"I'm dead if I don't."

"I heard what you was sayin'. What's this about you bein' there when they killed somebody, and about the bank?"

Cass told her, his voice broken in despair. "I didn't go to do it. I been an honest man all my life; you know that. It was Modock; he forced me into it."

"You don't think for a minute that he can let you leave here alive, knowin' what you do? He knows sooner or later you'd break down and tell somebody, then they'd come after him. Once he gets your name on them papers he wants, you're dead. We're all dead."

"Not you. He wants you."

"I'd as soon be dead. Anyway, he'd get tired of me, and then he'd have to kill me too because I know the whole story now."

The old man buried his face in his hands. "I never knowed it would end thisaway. I was so filled with hate for Blair Bishop, I'd of done anything Modock wanted me to." In a minute he looked up, a little hope in his eyes. "Maybe if we promised him we wouldn't ever say nothin' . . . maybe if we promised we'd leave this country and not ever come back within three hundred miles . . ."

"He won't let you leave here, or me," she said gravely. "He'll kill Allan first, and then you . . . and eventually me. The minute you sign them papers, it's over for all of us." She looked at Harley Mills, who slacked against the wall on the far side of the shed. Mills was drunk, but he had heard enough that alarm was beginning to reach him. He kept trying to focus his eyes on Owen Darby, who sat with pistol in his hand, listening and smiling to himself. Sunlight kept striking Mills in the face through one of the several big holes in the west wall. He would blink and move a little, but in a minute he would sag a little and the sun would hit him again.

The expression in Darby's face showed plainly that every word the girl said was true. Jessie spoke to Mills. "If you're not stupid drunk, Harley Mills, you better think a little bit about your own situation. Sooner or later Modock's goin' to decide maybe you've heard too much and seen too much too. Once he's got what he needs from you, you'll be in the same fix as the rest of us."

Darby snarled at her. "Shut up."

Jessie took a cloth from Allan's head and soaked it in a pan of water while she put a fresh wet cloth in its place. "And if I don't?"

"You may've got into Macy's blood, but you ain't got into mine."

Old Clarence looked fearfully at Darby. "You'd kill a woman?"

Darby raised the pistol a little, then lowered it. "Takes one bullet for a woman, same as for a man. I can buy all the woman I need in town for five dollars. This one wouldn't be no loss to me."

Clarence buried his face again. "Oh, God, little girl, what did I get you into?"

Macy Modock waited a long while before he came back into the shed. He had calculated on the wait to shatter Clarence Cass' nerves. He stood in the door, the afternoon sun ominously casting the shadow of his tall frame across the shed floor. "I got the papers laid out on the kitchen table. You ready, Clarence?"

From somewhere, Cass summoned strength to say, "Go to hell, Macy."

Macy Modock gave him a kick that sent him backward, arms flailing. Modock took a long stride and stood over him. "Sometimes I get awful short of patience, Clarence."

Clarence Cass drew up in pain, shaking his head. "I ain't signin'. I ain't signin'."

Darby stood up. "Why don't you go take yourself a drink, Macy? Let me argue with him a little."

Angrily Modock said, "Just don't kill him . . . quite." He turned on his heel.

Darby enjoyed his work. He kept it up until Jessie jumped from the unconscious boy's side and threw herself against Darby, striking at him with her fists and cursing him in language a girl wasn't supposed to know. Darby grabbed her shoulders and flung her roughly into the hay.

Harley Mills had sat bleary-eyed and fearful during the beating of the old ranchman. At the manhandling of the girl, he pushed to a wobbly stand and took a halting step forward. "Now you just looky here . . ."

Darby turned on him. "Sit down and shut

up, drunk. Take another slug of whiskey and don't pay no attention to what don't concern you."

Modock came back presently. He saw the girl first, disheveled, the hay clinging. His angry eyes cut dangerously toward Darby.

Darby said, "She come at me a-fightin'. I just shook a little sense into her, is all."

"She's mine, Owen, and you damn well better remember it." Modock leaned over and grasped the old ranchman's shirtfront. "Clarence . . ." He shook Cass, but he got little response. He let go, and the ranchman fell back. Modock straightened, speaking sharply to Darby. "I told you not to kill him. He ain't no good to me if he ain't in shape to sign his name."

"He ain't hurt. He's just a cowardly old man playin' possum on you."

Modock towered over Cass, hands on his hips. "Listen to me, Clarence. Don't pretend you can't hear me. I'll be back in a little while, and you better be ready to sign. Else I'll take a horse and a rope and I'll drag you up and down that brushy flat yonder."

Three of Modock's hands confronted him as he stepped out of the shed. Modock could see trouble in the way they looked at him. One had elected himself spokesman. "Macy, we don't like the way things is shapin' up."

Modock stiffened. "What's the matter with them?"

"First thing, you oughtn't to've sent Jim and Charlie out by theirselves with that herd the way you done. Maybe they wouldn't of gotten killed. And besides that, takin' land and cattle away from a big man like Blair Bishop is one thing. Beatin' the life out of a weak-backed old man like Clarence is somethin' else; we don't like the smell of it. And we don't like what you got in mind for that girl either. When you can buy more women than you'd know what to do with, we don't like you misusin' one."

Modock's hand was near the butt of his pistol. "Any one of you feel like he's man enough to stop me?"

The men looked at each other, then at Modock. "Maybe we can't stop you, but we sure don't aim to stay around and help you. We're goin' on, Macy."

Macy Modock boiled in frustration. He wanted to draw and shoot them like the slinking dogs that they were. But he knew it was unlikely he could beat all three. "Then go on, damn you. Run like a pack of rabbits. Ain't nobody needs you around here."

But as he watched them saddling their horses to leave, he felt the whole thing

196

beginning to trickle away between his fingers. He *did* need them. He needed the force they represented. He couldn't do this thing alone, just him and Darby. Damn them for cowards! Damn them for quitters! He watched them leave and trembled in helpless fury. He drew his pistol and nearly gave way to an urge to kill them all. But as the men rode, they were all turned in their saddles, watching him until they were well out of range.

Modock stared after them, the fierce anger burning unchecked. When they were beyond recall, he turned sharply and strode back into the shed. Roughly he yanked Cass to his feet. "I've pussyfooted all I'm goin' to. We're goin' into that house, Clarence, and you're signin' them papers if you do it with your last dyin' breath!" He flung Cass through the door. The old man went down on his knees, but Modock didn't let him stay there. Modock half carried, half dragged him to the house while Jessie Cass stood in the shed door and watched, her hands to her mouth. Harley Mills swayed with one hand braced back against the wall, sobering under the impact of violence. Owen Darby walked to the door and shoved the girl back. "Sit down!" he said roughly, and then stood in the doorway, a hard smile across his face as he watched the house and imagined what Modock was doing in there.

Modock pushed Clarence Cass toward the kitchen table where he had the deeds spread out. A pen lay atop the papers, and an ink bottle beside them. "Sign, Clarence. Sign them papers or I'll kill you where you stand!"

Clarence Cass sobbed aloud, because he could see death in Modock's fury . . . death whether he signed or whether he didn't. Modock struck him. "Sign!"

Cass sank into a chair. He reached for the pen, jabbing the point at the ink bottle without realizing he had to unscrew the top.

"Open it first, you stupid . . ."

Cass fumbled with the bottle, got the top off, then let the whole thing slip through his fingers. The bottle hit the floor rolling, the ink spilling. Before Modock could outrun it and pick it up, it was empty. It didn't have ink enough left to wet the pen. Modock hurled it against a wall, then turned and struck Cass again. "You'll sign if you have to do it in your own damned blood!"

Cass huddled in the chair, trembling like a cottonwood leaf. He said, "I think I know where there's another bottle."

"Get it!"

Cass pushed shakily to his feet. He walked

into the room where he customarily slept and swayed forward, catching himself on a battered old chest of drawers. He paused a moment, summoning strength, then pulled out the drawer. He reached into it, his hand hidden momentarily from Modock. When he turned, he held an old pistol in his hands. His eyes were desperate. He shrilled, "Die, Modock!" and pulled the trigger.

It clicked.

Modock couldn't risk the next one doing the same. His own pistol came up and leveled swiftly. Even as he squeezed the trigger, he knew he had lost this ranch.

The gun thundered. Clarence Cass was driven backward against the window. He fell through it and out in a shower of glass. He lay hanging, his knees bent across the windowsill, his arms slacked, his limp hands touching the ground outside.

Modock picked up the fallen pistol. He flipped open the cylinder and shouted aloud. "Empty!" He hurled it through the broken window, knowing Cass was dead, knowing that by grabbing up an empty gun he had wiped away all Modock's hopes of taking this land. Modock leaned out the window and cursed him and emptied his gun into the frail body.

At the shed, Owen Darby stood transfixed.

He had heard the commotion in the house, heard the shot and saw Cass fall backward through the window. He watched hypnotized as Modock fired again and again in fury and frustration.

Jessie Cass had known when her father went into that house he had little chance of leaving it alive. To her he was dead before she ever heard the first shot. She flinched, and she cried out, but she had already given up.

"It's Allan next," she rasped to Harley Mills, "and then you, and then me."

She pushed to her feet as the other shots began. Outside the shed, she could see Darby standing frozen, forgetting about the people in the shed because of his fascination in the scene at the house. He held the pistol loosely in his hand, forgotten in the excitement.

Her blood like ice, she stared at the pistol. Her hands flexed, and she considered her chances of running out and grabbing it. They were nil, for Darby's strength would be too much.

Harley Mills was sobering fast. From the pile of hay he took the pitchfork and staggered forward. Jessie saw what he was trying and knew he was in no condition to carry through. She wrested the fork from his hands, took a firm grip and rushed.

Darby heard. He turned, bringing up the pistol. She speared his hand with one of the sharp tines, and he let the weapon drop. She kicked it aside. Holding the bleeding hand, he stared at her a moment in rage, then rushed her. She dropped the butt end of the fork to the ground to brace it. The force of his rush carried him headlong into the tines.

Darby screamed and fought against the embedded fork. He managed somehow to pull it free. He staggered, holding his arms tight against his belly as he cried to Macy Modock for help. Jessie grabbed up the fallen pistol and rushed back into the shed.

Modock ran out of the house, eyes wide in confusion. He saw the staggering Darby and started toward him. In panic, holding the pistol in both hands, Jessie fired. She missed him by a long way, but she stopped him. He ran back around the house.

Darby kept crying out, staggering until loss of blood brought him to his knees. He called to Modock for help, but Modock was in no position to assist him.

Mills was cold sober now. Darby's cries chilled him.

"For God's sake, girl, shoot him. Put him out of his misery."

Milk-pale, Jessie shook her head. "I've used up one bullet. We may need all that's left."

In blind agony, Darby crawled up the tank dam and over toward the water that lay beyond the deep mud. Presently he went quiet. Jessie shuddered. "You watch that side of the shed and I'll watch this one," she told Mills. "We can't let Modock slip up on us."

Modock waited awhile before he showed himself, calling from the corner of the house. "Girl, you can't hold out in there by yourself. That boy's no help to you, or that drunk. You throw the pistol out here where I can see it. There won't no harm come to you. Wouldn't be no reason for it anymore."

Her throat was dry and tight, and her heart throbbed in fear. She didn't answer. She held the pistol in both hands and braced it against the doorframe, sighting down the barrel.

Emboldened, Modock stepped out a little farther. "Girl, you better listen to me. I got more time and patience than you have."

She squeezed the trigger. Through the smoke she saw splinters fly from the corner of the house. Modock rushed back out of sight.

"Would've been better," Mills said, "if

Darby had died here in the door. We could've got the cartridges out of his belt."

Jessie nodded, her hands trembling as she lowered the smoking pistol. This was a six-shooter. She had fired two shots. Provided that Darby had kept it fully loaded — which she was sure he would — she had four shots left.

Modock leaned out from the corner of the house and fired deliberately at the shed. Jessie dropped to the floor as the bullets smacked into the wall over her head. When she had time to think, she realized Modock must have purposely aimed high.

He still wanted her alive, she knew. He was trying to scare her, and he was doing a good job of it.

She raised up, her instinct to fire back at him, but she knew the shot would be wasted. He was probably trying to lure her into doing just that. She sank to her knees, the pistol across her lap. Warm tears ran down her face.

"Girl," Harley Mills said, "you better let me have that gun."

She looked up at him and saw he was shaking. "No," she said, "you got way too much whiskey in you. You'd wind up killin' us instead of Modock."

Presently Modock fired again, still aiming

high. Jessie ducked involuntarily and cried out as splinters showered down. She heard a horse running excitedly in a corral behind the shed. Through a crack in the wall she looked at the house, and a fresh hope began to rise.

"Mister Mills, he's still behind the house, or in it. He can't get away from it very well without me seein' him. That's his horse behind the shed makin' all the commotion. You could catch that horse and saddle it without exposin' yourself to Modock none. There's a wagon behind the shed too. You could go down into the draw, fetch up the team, and we could hitch it to the wagon. We could load Allan into the wagon and light out of here in a dead run. Modock bein' afoot, there wouldn't be no way he could stop us once we started."

Mills shook his head fearfully. "I don't know. If he was to ever get a clear shot at me . . ."

"He won't, if you watch how you handle yourself. Anyway, I'll keep the house covered."

"Girl, you can't even hit that house, much less hit Modock."

She flung all her anger at him. "Have you got a drop of red blood left in your veins, or has it all gone to whiskey?"

He dropped his chin. The violence had largely cleared his mind, though his reflexes were still not coordinated. "I didn't come out here to get killed."

"You came out here to lie your way into some whiskey money. Maybe you've learned now you don't get nothin' you don't pay for. Are you goin' out there and catch that horse?"

Slump-shouldered, Mills took a bridle from a hook and a rope from a saddle that had belonged to Darby. Jessie went back to watching the house. She could hear the horse running around and around the pen and could hear the swish of the loop as Mills tried several times to catch him and missed. But finally from the sounds she knew he had caught the horse and was saddling him. She stepped to the shed's corral door long enough to see Mills swing into the saddle. She called, "You bring back that team, do you hear?"

Mills bare-heeled the horse into a lope and bent low over the saddle as he left the pen. He angled in such a way that he kept the shed between him and the house until he was out of range. Jessie went back to her vigil by the front door and waited for Mills to return. She felt of Allan's forehead and found it hot. Allan mumbled feverishly, unaware of what was going on.

"We'll be out of here directly," she murmured. "Just as soon as Mills gets back with that team."

Time moved rapidly enough at first as in her mind she followed Mills down into the draw. She knew where the wagon team usually grazed, and how long it would take Mills to get down there. She visualized his picking them up and starting back toward the barn. She followed his progress all the way.

"He ought to be comin' just about now," she said to the unconscious boy. "We'll hear him any minute."

The minutes ticked by slowly then, no sound coming. Maybe the team had grazed farther than usual, she tried to tell herself. Even a horse doesn't do the same thing every day; even a horse likes variety. She allowed the extra time, mentally beginning over, giving Mills a fresh start back from the draw. Still he didn't come.

For a long time she resisted the obvious: he wasn't coming back. But finally the realization forced itself upon her against her will. For the first time she broke down and openly cried.

XV

It was dusk now. Jessie knew that only so long as there was still light could she keep Modock pinned behind that house. Even then, there was no way to be absolutely sure. He could walk away, carefully keeping the house between him and the shed, and she would not see him. If he walked far enough to lose himself in the brush, he could get completely away, or he could circle back and come up on her from behind.

But Modock was still at the house. She heard him call. "Mills is gone now, girl. That boy can't help you, so it's just me and you."

She didn't answer him. He waited a little, then said, "You can't hold out. Sooner or later you got to give up. Do it now and I promise I won't do that boy no more harm. You and me, we'll ride out of here together."

She knew he was lying. For a while there had been some possible advantage to him in keeping Allan alive. Now there was none. She knew his hatred for Blair Bishop was so intense that he would kill Allan simply for revenge on Allan's father. And when he was done, he would still carry Jessie away with him. There was no bargaining with a man who knew no honor.

"You stay away, Modock," she cried. "You stay away from us."

He showed himself, and in a moment of desperation she fired again. Instantly she realized she had made a mistake.

That was it: he was trying to lure her into using up her cartridges. Once she had done that, all he had to do was walk in and take her.

He waited a time, then called to her again. "It's up to you, girl. I ain't goin' to put up with this all night. If I have to, I'll kill that boy."

To make his point, he fired at the shed. She saw the thin wood wall crack where the bullet struck, very little above Allan's cot. Modock knew the position where Allan lay. If he made up his mind to it, he could fire through the wall and kill him. And if a pistol wouldn't do it, there were a couple of rifles in the house at Modock's disposal.

Jessie took Allan's feverish hand and stared at him. She ran her fingers through his tousled hair. "If I move you," she said, "that wound is liable to break open and bleed some more. If I don't move you, he'll kill you sure. I got to do it, Allan. Try to help me if you can. I got to do it."

She didn't think her words ever got through to him. She reached under his shoulders and tried to lift him. He was too heavy. She could drag him off the cot, but then she wouldn't be able to keep him from falling, and that would hurt him for certain. The big problem was to ease him somehow to the floor. She mulled over it a moment, then reached across him with both hands, lifting the far edge of the cot, tipping it gradually toward her, pressing her body against his to keep him from falling. The lifting was heavy till she had the cot tipped halfway up; then the problem was to prevent the cot from falling too fast and Allan from tumbling. She held the cot most of the way. By the time it became too heavy for her, Allan was almost in her lap. He slid gently, and she had him. She cradled him in her arms a moment, pressing her cheek against him. He mumbled fevered words that had no meaning.

Modock fired again, and she saw a ragged hole appear in the wall where Allan had been. Modock had a rifle now. He had given up fooling around. Jessie lay on the ground, her arms around Allan, and began laboriously dragging him away. She crawled a few inches at a time toward the back of the shed, while Macy Modock methodically sent slug after slug tearing through the wall.

If she hadn't moved Allan, he would be dead by now.

She didn't stop dragging until she had him almost to the back wall. She looked around for anything she could pile up between him and the wall that faced the house. She flung down Darby's saddle and one of her father's and also her own, knowing all of them together might not be enough to stop a rifle bullet. She piled up the horse collars and the harness and several sacks of grain that had been bought for the chickens.

"He's dead now, girl," Modock shouted. "No point in you tryin' to protect him anymore. You come on out here and throw that gun away."

The clapboard walls were shoddily constructed, like everything else on the Cass place. Jessie could watch the house through spaces between the boards. She saw Modock step out experimentally in the dusk, inviting her to fire at him. She wanted to, but she resisted. She held her breath, taking in a gasp of air once in a while, then holding while she watched Modock. He waited a while for her to fire then moved a few feet forward and stopped again.

"Girl," he called, "do you hear me?"

She made no reply. He took a few more steps, and she could see his face clearly. In his changing expressions she could almost read his mind. He was suddenly becoming fearful he had hit her with some of those shots intended for Allan Bishop. He came forward again, halting occasionally, still not sure.

"Girl, are you all right? I want you to answer me."

The closer he came, the surer he seemed to be that she had been hit, and the less caution he showed. Jessie sat up, holding the pistol firmly in both hands, arms extended stiffly. She aimed at the doorframe, waiting for the moment he would step through into full sight.

She couldn't see him now, but she could hear the slow tread of his boots. She caught a deep breath and held it.

He came through the door, pistol ready. "Girl?"

He couldn't see her immediately, not in the darkness at the back of the shed. His gaze went to the overturned cot and the blankets.

Jessie saw him over the sights, took a firm grip on the pistol and pulled the trigger. Modock jerked, and she fired again. Black smoke billowed, hiding him from her view.

She heard him cry out in surprise and pain, and she heard his footsteps running again across the yard. She dropped onto her stomach and peered out through the spaces. She saw him half running, half hopping as he disappeared behind the house.

She hadn't killed him, but she had drawn blood. He would think a long time before he came again.

And Jessie knew she would have to think a long time before she fired at him, for the next shot would be her last. She had but one bullet left.

Allan whispered, "Jessie." She turned quickly to him and saw his eyelids flicker a little. The gunfire had stirred him at last. She put her arms around him and lay against him and put her cheek to his burning forehead. "Lie easy," she said, "just lie easy. Everything will be all right."

Then it was dark and she could see no more. All she could do now was lie here by Allan and listen fearfully. With the darkness came all the night sounds of the crickets and the night birds and the far-off bawling of a cow in search of its calf. But no noise came from the house. Jessie listened intently, trying to separate each sound and analyze it, looking for menace in the light summer wind that rustled the leaves, chilling at the sudden yip of a roaming coyote far out on the prairie.

The dark hours dragged by. She had cried some at first, but now the tears were dried. Hands that had been cold-sweaty against the gunbutt held it now as firmly as ever, but they too were dry. She no longer stirred at every sound; she had listened to them so long that she knew now which ones were natural.

When Modock came — and she was still sure he would — he wouldn't find her in panic again. He would find her ready. With the one bullet she had left, she would kill him if she could. And if she didn't kill him, she would force him to kill her. He wasn't going to have her . . . not alive.

She had no way of keeping up with time. She didn't particularly want to, for she felt sure Modock would make his move before daylight came again, and she was not eager to see the night end. But she knew midnight must have come and gone when she heard the sounds. She pushed to her elbows, listening, trying to pin down their source.

She doubted Modock would try the front

door again. Perhaps not the back one, either, for he would not want to be as plain a target as he had been before. She expected him to slip up to the wall, for it had plenty of holes and cracks that he could see through without unnecessarily exposing himself to fire. Probably he would try to wound her just enough to put her out of the fight. A wounded girl was better than a dead one, he would probably figure. She lay holding her breath, listening.

The sounds were louder. He must be easing closer. She took a deep breath and then held it again.

Where was he? For God's sake, where was he?

Then she recognized the sounds: horses, running. It wasn't Modock! It was somebody else, somebody coming.

"Allan," she cried, "do you hear it? They're comin' to help us."

She judged that the horses were in the draw now. They would be here in minutes.

She heard something else, too — a man afoot, hurrying across the yard. Modock was coming. This was his last chance, and he was going to use it. He wasn't making any effort to slip up on her. He didn't have time. She knew he was coming straight for the door. She sat up, bringing the pistol into line, both hands gripping it steady. When he came through that door she would get him. This time she wouldn't miss.

The dark shape suddenly hurled itself at her. Crying out involuntarily, she squeezed the trigger. The flash seemed to light up the whole shed, and she saw the shape fall.

But it didn't fall like a man. It fell limp and lay flat.

In anguish, Jessie realized Modock had tricked her out of her last shot. He had flung a blanket through that door, and in the darkness she had thrown away her last chance. He stood now where the blanket had appeared.

"That's all of it, girl."

Not quite all. She threw the empty pistol at him in desperation and pushed to her feet. She didn't wait for him to come to her; she rushed at him, pummeling him with her fists, crying out in her hatred of him. He put his pistol away, grabbed her hands and pushed her back. When she came at him again, he lashed out with his fist and caught her chin. She fell to her knees, stunned.

"You're a fighter," he rasped, "I'll admit that. I just wish I'd of thought about that blanket trick hours ago. Then I'd of had some time with you. Now I got no time left, and no patience. You've caused me all the grief I'm goin' to take." He drew the pistol and shoved it at her. "Give me one more bit of trouble and I'll kill that boy yonder. Then, if I decide to — and I may — I'll kill you too."

The horses loped into the yard. A deep voice called out.

"Allan! Allan, boy, where you at?"

Helpless to resist anymore, Jessie crawled to Allan and put her arms around him. His eyes were open, and he was trying to clear them. "Jessie?" he said, his voice only a whisper.

"Yes, Allan, it's me."

"Jessie, what's goin' on?"

"Your dad is here. He's outside. But Modock is in here with us, and he's got a gun."

From the sounds, Jessie could tell the men were dismounting in the yard and spreading out. She recognized Blair Bishop's voice calling again. "Allan! Jessie! Are you-all here?"

Jessie cried, "Stay away, Mister Bishop! It's Modock!"

Modock pulled back into the shadows, nearer Jessie and Allan. "Like she says, Bishop, we're all in here together. Why don't you come on in . . . if you want this boy killed?"

There was silence for a moment, then

Bishop said, "Modock, whatever quarrel you got, it's with me, not with my boy or that girl."

"That's right, Bishop, it's you and me. It's always been you and me."

"Well, then," Bishop called, "what do you want?"

"Just you, Bishop, just you."

"You got me, if you'll let them kids go. What do you want me to do?"

"Make them men of yours git away . . . plumb away. Just you is all I want to see out there. Just you and two horses . . . one for you and one for me."

Jessie could hear Blair Bishop quietly giving orders and the men pulling back.

Modock said: "You give them orders that I get to ride out of here clean. And you're goin' with me."

"They heard you," Bishop said. "It's the same as an order from me."

Modock moved closer to the door, satisfying himself that the other riders had remounted and moved back. "All right, Bishop, you come closer where I can look at you."

Jessie could hear Bishop's footsteps and made out the heavy shape of him, dark against the open door. Modock gloated. "Well, it didn't turn out the way I figured

217

on, but I got this one thing I was after. You did come to *me.* Drop your pistol."

Bishop raised his hands a little. "Ain't got one, Macy. These old hands, I couldn't use one if I carried it, so I don't bother myself packin' the weight."

Jessie became aware of a slight scurrying noise at the back wall. She looked around, mouth open in wonder. She saw the barrel of a shotgun poke through a knothole a little above her head. She saw it move up and down, its holder outside trying vainly to draw a bead on Modock.

At the bottom of the wall was a hole big enough for a cat to move through. Quietly she leaned forward and eased her hand out. The shotgun muzzle quickly disappeared. She felt the touch of cold steel, and then the touch of fingers, gently pressing the shotgun into her hand. Carefully, her eyes on Modock, she began pulling the shotgun into the barn.

Modock was busy glorying over getting Blair Bishop into a trap. He had his back turned to her. She kept pulling the shotgun until it was clearly inside, then cautiously brought it up. She almost had a bead on Modock when Blair Bishop stepped fully into the barn.

Her heart sank. She couldn't fire without

Bishop sharing the blast.

Bishop was saying: "I'll go with you, Macy. But first I got to see about my boy. I got to be sure he's alive."

Modock backed away, giving Bishop room to pass by. But it wasn't enough room that Jessie could get a clear shot. And she knew that when he turned to let his gaze follow Bishop, he would see the shotgun in her hands. She lowered it, laying it lengthwise beside Allan Bishop, hoping Modock wouldn't spot it in the darkness.

"He's alive," Modock said. "That girl has kept him alive in spite of all I could do. But go see for yourself. Then you and me are ridin' out of here, Bishop. You're my ticket for a free passage."

Blair Bishop limped over and dropped to one knee. "Allan?"

Allan whispered, "Dad." Bishop rasped, "Thank God." He raised his eyes to Jessie and looked at her a minute. "And thank you, girl."

He reached out for her hand. She caught his fingers and gently guided them down to the shotgun. She saw the surprise show for a second in his face before he covered it. Bishop bent over as if to hug his son.

"You've seen him," Modock said. "Now come on."

"I'm comin'," Blair replied, his back turned to Modock as he slowly arose, holding the shotgun against his body.

Jessie flattened herself beside Allan. Blair turned, getting as good a grip on the shotgun as his stiff hands would let him.

Confident of Blair's helplessness, Modock had let his pistol sag. He saw the shotgun too late. Giving a startled cry, he tried to bring up the pistol. Bishop didn't give him time. The blast knocked Modock to the floor. He rolled halfway through the door, gathered one knee up as if to push again to his feet, then slumped forward and died there.

Blair Bishop said, "Harley Mills didn't have it in him to go back with the team, once he got clear of the place. But he did work up enough courage to come and tell me. I reckon that took some guts just in itself."

He stood at the foot of Allan's bed in the Bishop house, looking at a weary Jessie Cass, who ought to have been off somewhere asleep but wouldn't leave Allan's side. She sat in a chair by the bed and watched Allan.

"I don't know what these boys are comin' to, this day and time," Blair went on. "There wouldn't none of this of wound up the way it did if my two boys had listened to what I told them. I tried to raise them different, but they're just plain contrary. Got it from their mother, God bless her. Allan first. I told him to stay home and not be runnin' off to you, but he went anyway, and you see what become of him for it. Then Billy . . . when Harley Mills come by, I told Billy to stay home. He was too young to get into a fight like this, and I didn't want to lose *two* boys. He come anyhow. And when I told him to move out of the way with the others, he took the shotgun and run for the back of the shed instead.

"No, seems like I can't tell them boys nothin' anymore. And it's probably a good thing."

Jessie nodded wearily, agreeing with him, though she was plainly too tired to know half of what he said. It looked to Blair as if she would drop off to sleep in that chair, and maybe he ought to go away and let her. But he had one more thing he wanted to say. "I never been wrong but very few times in my life, and I hope I ain't never wrong again. But I was wrong about you, girl. I'll make it up to you, any way an old man can find to do it."

"You just give me Allan, Mister Bishop,

and that's all the makin' up you'll ever have to do."

"He's yours. He ought to be up and goin' again pretty soon. September's just around the corner. I feel like we'll get a good rain then, and everything'll look better. How would you like a nice big September weddin', girl?"

She smiled. "I'd *like* a September weddin'. In the rain."

ABOUT THE AUTHOR

Elmer Kelton of San Angelo, Texas, is a seven-time winner of the Spur Award, has earned four Western Heritage Awards from the National Cowboy Hall of Fame, and was named the greatest Western author of all time by Western Writers of America in 1995.

The employees of Thorndike Press hope you have enjoyed this Large Print book. All our Thorndike and Wheeler Large Print titles are designed for easy reading, and all our books are made to last. Other Thorndike Press Large Print books are available at your library, through selected bookstores, or directly from us.

For information about titles, please call:
  (800) 223-1244

or visit our Web site at:
  www.gale.com/thorndike
  www.gale.com/wheeler

To share your comments, please write:
  Publisher
  Thorndike Press
  295 Kennedy Memorial Drive
  Waterville, ME 04901